I0613297

THE SECRET FILES

OF

SCOTLAND YARD:

The Origin of Detective Angus O'Connor-McCurr

WRITTEN BY:

REBECCA DAVIS

This book is dedicated to the two who supported me the most in my journey to become an author. Thank you so much to Professor Niles Haich. Thank you for never giving up on me even when I started to give up on myself and for pushing me to keep writing when others thought I shouldn't. And a great big thank you to my Mom for being my editor, advisor and cheerleader. I would not have been able to do any of this without you.

CASE FILE #00001

CASE MANAGER: BRIANNA BAIRD

LEAD AGENT: GORDON McCurr

SUBJECT: Angus O'Connor

It was a dark night nearly nine years ago when I first laid eyes on the boy. The pain in his gaze was raw, deep, and haunting, a type of suffering that only someone who had witnessed something as terrible as murder could show. It was unsettling to see in one so young. I had just received a phone call from a house located on Kenmure Avenue. The caller reported hearing gunshots from the residence across the street. My heart raced as I recognized the address. I knew that house. I had visited it on more than one occasion to meet with the O'Connor Family.

It felt like yesterday when I spoke with Fergus O'Connor about his newborn son, Angus. That baby boy was still a

small child the last time I had seen
him, just a little over four years old.
I remembered our conversation about his
father's mysterious disappearance
several years earlier. The pain
surrounding that family lingered in the
air like a dark, foreboding shadow. I
never imagined that night would haunt
me forever.

As I stood there, memories of the
O'Connor family flooded back. I could
picture their faces— their warmth, hear
the joy in their laughter. But in that
moment, everything changed. The dark
night and the chilling report of
gunshots pulled me into a reality that
I feared, one that I did not want to
confront. The weight of the night
pressed in around me. I had to act.

Three things caught my attention
when I stepped into their small home.
The first was a body that I quickly
recognized as belonging to Iris

O'Connor. She lay lifeless, surrounded
by an unsettling calm that filled the
dark corridor. The second was that the
pool of blood surrounding her had been
smeared and distorted. Upon taking a
closer look, I realized that written in
blood next to her were strange
markings, markings that appeared to
hold importance but were impossible to
decipher. I have included them in this
report in hopes that perhaps in the
future they can be identified: ᛋᚺᛗ ᚲᛏᛗᛈ
ᛏᛟᛟ ᛗᚾᚲᚺ, ᚾᛏᛞ ᚺᛗᛈ ᛋᛁᛏᛗᛣᚲᛗ ᛈᛏᛋ ᛣᛟᛏ ᛗᛣᛉᚾᚷᚺ.
Though they could just be the insane
scribbles of the one who committed this
crime. The third and final thing that
stood out to me was a young boy huddled
in the corner. My heart sank as I
realized that he must be Angus, her
only son. He appeared terrified, his
face wet with tears that streamed down
his cheeks. His eyes were fixed on the
still frame of his mother, unable to

look away from the reality that
surrounded him. The atmosphere was
thick with grief, a silent witness to
the tragic scene unfolding before me.
In that moment, the weight of loss hung
like a heavy curtain in the air, while
the boy's quiet sobs echoed through the
small space, marking the depth of his
sorrow.

The hours passed slowly as we
waited for permission to move her body
to the morgue. We needed to establish
the approximate time of death. It was
also crucial to identify the type of
gun that fired the bullet that ended
more than just a woman's life. The air
was tight with tension and sorrow,
filling the room where we stood so
completely it was hard to breathe.

While this process unfolded, my
mind turned to the little boy left
behind. He was shattered, a small
figure tossed overboard in a sea of

confusion. He stood there, eyes wide with fear and uncertainty. He did not fully grasp what had happened; all he knew was that the world around him had shifted dramatically, and he could sense it. The reality of the situation loomed over me as a darkness enveloped him, leaving him to struggle with the weight of what had happened.

There were only a few details left to handle before I could go home. The most pressing was the need to figure out what to do with the grieving child beside me. His need for comfort resonated deeply with me, and how could it not, me being an orphan myself. I could not leave him there alone, lost, afraid of what might happen next. I had to ensure that he was cared for and had someone to turn to amidst the chaos. The stakes were high, and time was running out.

Because Angus was still a child and had no legal guardian, he faced a difficult future. The authorities above had decided to send him to a place that was meant to serve as an orphanage. Though to note, I would have taken him in myself, had the law allowed. Yet my unpredictable work hours made it impossible for me to promise him stability; I could not guarantee my presence in his life.

Angus had already endured so much. He had witnessed the horrifying murder of his mother, an experience no child should ever have to face. The pain from that moment would linger in his young mind and fester in ways we could not predict. Sending him away to a place that would not understand him felt wrong. It felt like I would be abandoning him all over again. My decision weighed heavily on me. It was clear that Angus needed care, but I worried about his future. Life was cruel, and I hoped that wherever he ended up, he would find kindness and safety. I imagined him in a warm place where he could heal and grow, far from the horrors he had seen. But that was not my decision to make.

Another challenge lay before me that required just as much attention. Angus was a witness. He had witnessed a horrific murder. And to intensify the trauma, the victim was none other than his own mother. It took nearly an hour to coax Angus out of the dark, damp corner where he had taken his refuge. He sat there, lost, afraid, struggling to come to terms with what he had just seen. Each moment stretched on, filled with fear and disbelief, making it hard for him to move. The task of pulling him into the light felt monumental as I tried to support him through his darkest hour.

ᗱHM ᴄ𝈁MP ↑ᗡᗷ
ᗺ∏ᴄᕼ, Ϝ𝈁⬨ ᕼMᖇ
ᗱIᒋM𝈁ᴄM PϜᗱ
𝈁ᗝ↑ Mᕼᗷᘉᗡᕼ.

CASE FILE # 000002

CASE MANAGER: BRIANNA BAIRD

LEAD AGENT: GORDON MCCURR

SUBJECT: Angus O'Connor

The drive to Scotland Yard's
headquarters was enveloped in a thick,
almost unbearable silence. The silence
itself spoke volumes about the gravity
of the situation we were about to face.
Inside the car, the weight of the
moment pressed down on me. I needed to
collect the young boy's statement and
see if he could identify the person
responsible for the tragedy that had
shattered his world. Upon arriving at
the station house, I stepped into my
workspace, the familiar surroundings
suddenly feeling more daunting than
usual. The tension in the air was
palpable, and my mind raced with
thoughts. I quickly sought out a
constable, asking him to look after

Angus until I returned. I felt a pang of guilt leaving the recently orphaned boy in the care of a stranger, someone whose name I didn't even know. Yet, the task in front of me held a vital sense of importance.

There were details in this case that troubled me, bits of information that did not align with the limited evidence we had gathered. My priority was to speak with the coroner at the morgue across the way. The facts were elusive, and I hoped that by seeking answers there, I could shed light on the shadows surrounding the case. The boy deserved clarity as much as the killer deserved justice. With a heavy heart, I steeled myself to uncover the truth, even as I left him in uncertain hands.

As I made my way back to headquarters, thoughts raced through my mind. The coroner's words about the weapon lingered. It was identified as a pistol of Belgian origin; the bullet was only seven millimeters, and yet the damage felt so much more destructive. The image of the bullet flashed in my mind as I navigated the busy streets. Upon entering the building, I was immediately struck by the sight of the constable I had left with Angus. He looked visibly shaken, his face pale and tense. The chatter in the room faded to a dull roar as Angus's ragged breathing tore through the aire. My heart hammered against my rib cage, an urgent drumbeat of alarm. Pushing through the bullpen, I quickly knelt beside him.

"Angus!" I called, attempting to cut through his rising panic. I knelt quickly and placed my hands firmly on his trembling shoulders. His skin was ashen, and his face was slick with sweat. His panicked eyes were unfocused and glassy.

"Angus, hey, look at me, kid." My voice was low, an attempt at projecting a steadiness I wasn't sure I felt. He only shook harder, his head lolling sideways as his breath tore from his throat in harsh, shallow gasps that reminded me of the sound of ripping fabric.

"I… ca… I can't…" A choked sob escaped him as the words caught in his throat.

"You're safe, Angus. Right here, there isn't anywhere safer than in this building," I watched as uncertainty flickered in his gaze as I tightened my grasp on his shoulders, gently shaking him in hopes of giving him a physical anchor. " I need you to listen to me, just for a moment, okay?"

Angus shivered violently, unable to speak, his whole body coiled in terror as he turned his gaze towards me.

"Good. Now I want you to take a slow, deep breath with me." Angus shook his head. "It's okay, just copy me. Can you do that? In through your nose." I exaggerated my own slow, deep inhale, my chest rising visibly.

Angus tried, only managing a sharp, choked inhale, barely a gasp.

"Good. That's a start. Now, hold it… just for a count of four. One… Two… Three… Four… Now slowly let it out through your mouth, like you're blowing out a candle." I demonstrated, releasing my breath in a long, soft hiss.

Angus let out a shaky, desperate exhale, his shoulders still heaving.

"You've got it, Angus. Let's do it again… you're safe, kid. Just keep breathing."

It took almost fifteen minutes for
me to calm his breathing until I felt
assured he would not pass out. I
watched for signs of relief on his
face. When I was confident in his
composure, I decided it was time to
step outside. I gently guided the
constable from the room into the
hallway, keeping my voice low and
steady. The gas lights flickered
quietly overhead as we stood there,
tension still heavy in the air. I
turned to him, asking what had
happened. The constable seemed shaken
as he spoke.

"We were sitting quietly when the
Chief Inspector shouted at a constable
in his path, slamming a file on the
desk, which echoed throughout the room.
Angus's face lost its color as a stark
look of terror overshadowed the somber
look that he had shown since he arrived
with you, McCurr." The Constable

swallowed thickly, "He started shaking and I wasn't sure what to do…" he trailed off.

I thought back to how I found him in the house earlier that night and remembered something I had run across in another case of mine, where the victim had survived but was irrevocably scarred by what had occurred. The symptoms were similar.

I quickly came to the understanding that Angus, a boy of only twelve, had witnessed something deeply disturbing. This event had left its mark on him, creating emotional scars that, if left untreated, would escalate into severe issues later on. The trauma he experienced was evident. When I stepped back into the bustling room filled with people, the weight of my situation hit me hard. I realized that my challenges extended beyond just being a potential witness to a murder. I was faced with a terrified child who was completely lost in the chaos surrounding him. He had no grasp of the reality unfolding, and that added another layer of complexity to the case. I needed to tread carefully. The psychological effects on a young mind can be profound, and understanding his state was essential for dealing with the situation effectively.

I gently but firmly pulled Angus away from the chaos of the room and guided him to a quieter corner where he could sit down. His eyes were filled with confusion and hurt, and I struggled to find the right words to reach him. For a moment, I just stared at him, feeling helpless and unsure of what to say. My mind raced, trying to think of what he needed to hear, what might somehow comfort or make sense of this pain. Then, suddenly, it all clicked in my mind, and I knew what I

had to tell him. As I looked into his
eyes, my heart ached sharply. I looked
at him, the weight of my message forced
the words to catch in my throat, a knot
of dread tightening in my chest. I took
a breath, steeling myself.

"There is something I need to tell
you about your mother, Angus," I began,
my voice softer than I had intended.
Angus looked up at me, a flicker of
apprehension reflecting in his eyes.

"What... what is it?" he questioned,
his voice trembling.

"Your mother... she's been taken from
you," I explained, the words feeling
inadequate and even brutal. "She's
gone."

I watched as his face tightened, a
subtle shift that spoke volumes as the
realization crossed his face. His eyes
glimmered with unshed tears, searching
my gaze for any hint of a different
truth.

"Gone?" he repeated in a raw voice.

"Yes," I confirmed, my voice trembled despite my effort to keep it level. "There's no way to bring her back. I am so sorry." The finality of my statement hung heavy in the air. His face was stone, as his eyes were streaked with a pain so dark and profound it was almost too much for me to witness. It was like a deep wound that refused to heal.

What truly broke me was the way he responded. When I finished speaking, he looked away for a second, then whispered in a quiet, broken voice that I should bring her back. Not with anger or frustration, just a desperate plea, almost a plea for a miracle. His words hung heavy in the air. It was clear he held onto hope that somehow, no matter how impossible, I could fix what had been lost. When I told him that it wasn't possible, that we couldn't undo what had been done, the look in his eyes betrayed his heart. His face fell, and in that instant, I saw the deep well of sorrow and longing in his eyes. That simple look told me everything I needed to know—how much he loved Iris and how much he wanted her back, no matter the cost. Seeing that, feeling that pain, I couldn't help but feel a mix of sorrow and helplessness. Sometimes, words aren't enough. They can't ease the ache of losing someone you love, no matter how hard you try.

I knelt down once more to Angus and gently explained, "Your mum, she's in heaven now, little man; God needed her home. She may not be here right now, but she's in Heaven. Your mama was a God fearing woman, and I know she was raising you with the bible. Do you remember John 11:25-26?"

Angus nodded, tears leaking from the corners of his eyes. "That's the one with Mary and Martha. Where Jesus says 'I am the resurrection and the life. The one who believes in me will live, even though they die; and whoever lives by believing in me will never die.' Right?"

I nodded, "That's right Angus, hold on to that."

When I finished talking to him, he took a deep breath and I asked if he remembered what had happened, if he knew who was there, or what he saw. He told me only fragments—how all he saw was a dark, shadowy figure in the room. He described this figure as faceless, no features or expressions, just a looming silhouette. He remembered that this figure was pointing a gun directly at his mother. There was no clear face, no words—just that moment frozen in his mind. Then, he heard a loud, sharp sound, like a gunshot breaking the silence. After that, he fell to the floor. His mother was lying motionless, her body limp and still, on the ground where she had collapsed. That was all he could remember with any clarity—the dark figure, the gunshot, and his mother unconscious or worse. These memories haunted him, but they came in fragments, making it hard for him to piece everything together clearly.

As I looked at him more closely, I realized just how drained he was. His face was pale, his eyes glassy, and he was trembling. He was barely able to stand on his own, his body sagging. I knew he was not just emotionally shattered but physically exhausted, almost to the point of collapsing. The toll of the trauma was clear. I understood he wouldn't survive much longer if he stayed like this. I had to make a tough choice. I knew where he needed to go—and it was to the orphanage, a place he could get help and be safe. But I hesitated at first. Part of me wanted to take him somewhere else, to shelter him or find some other solution. Still, deep down, I knew he had no other options. He couldn't stay with me; I wasn't able to care for him long-term. His future depended on getting him to that orphanage, where staff could help him heal and find stability. It was a hard decision, but I understood it was the only way forward. The images of his mother, the silence after the shot, and his exhausted state all pushed me to act quickly—there was no time to waste.

CASE FILE #000003

CASE MANAGER: BRIANNA BAIRD

LEAD AGENT: GORDON McCurr

SUBJECT: Angus O'Connor

It was a long, tiring journey to reach the Smyllum Park Orphanage. What should have been a straightforward two-hour ride turned into something much longer. We started the trip by riding on horseback, guiding our tired animals along the dirt paths that wound through the quiet countryside. The sun had barely risen when we set out, and by the time we reached our destination, the hours had slipped away. As daylight faded into night, we transferred to a buggy to cover the last stretch. The bumpy ride added to the fatigue, and the trip now stretched into three long hours. The night grew darker, and with each passing minute, the eerie atmosphere of the place seemed to deepen.

When we finally arrived, the clock showed it was nearly one in the morning. The

orphanage loomed ahead, shrouded in shadows
and looking even more unsettling than I
remembered. Its dark silhouette seemed to
swallow the faint glow of the distant stars.
We approached the gate, a large metal fence
that encircled the property. The gate itself
looked old and rusted, creaking softly as it
swung open with a groan. Standing there, I
couldn't help but feel a strange urge to
gather him in and shield him from this
place. Yet, deep down, I knew this was the
best shelter for him, even if the sight of
the orphanage sent a chill crawling down my
spine. The ominous feeling only grew
stronger as we drew closer. The wind seemed
to whisper through the trees, making their
trunks sway and creak like tired old beings
protesting the silence. Every gust rattled
their branches, casting strange shadows
across the ground. The trees didn't stay
still; they seemed to groan and sway as if
alive, adding a ghostly sound to the night's
quiet. Overhead, the shrill cries of ravens

cut through the darkness, piercing the stillness like sharp needles. Their caws echoed eerily around the orphanage, giving the entire place a haunting ambience. It was a scene that felt frozen in time, a place that held stories of sorrow and secrets. The air was thick with a sense of loneliness and mystery, making the orphanage not just a building, but a symbol of somber history and silent suffering.

With a loud, sharp knock against the heavy, solid oak doors, we waited patiently on the other side. The sound echoed through the quiet hallway, piercing the stillness like a signal for action. We stood silently, the sense of anticipation hanging thick in the air. The heavy oak door swung inward, revealing a woman who seemed to be carved from practicality itself. Her dark hair was pulled into a knot so tight it looked painful, her face was free of any artifice. She was, on the whole, remarkably serene for her serious appearance. She wore a simple

dark robe that did nothing to soften her
appearance, and her gaze, as it landed on me
and Angus, was direct and unwavering.

I took a deep breath, bolstering myself
as the cool night air was sharp against my
lungs. Angus stood beside me and looked
younger than his twelve years as he wrapped
himself tighter in the blanket that one of
the constables had found for him. His small
presence was a stark reminder of the weight
I felt with my decision to leave him.

"Good evening," I began, my voice more
strained than I had hoped given the
importance of this introduction. "I'm
Detective Gordon McCurr. I apologize for the
lateness of the hour, but this is an urgent
situation." I gestured softly to Angus,
"This is Angus O'Connor."

Her eyes, dark and intelligent, were
fixed on me, prompting me to continue
without further preamble. Her expression was
oddly unreadable, almost like a blank canvas
of professional calm.

"Angus's mother was… tragically murdered this evening," I stated, the words tasting bitter on my tongue. "There's no one. No family… And he is in significant danger if he stays anywhere else." I leaned in slightly, lowering my voice, though I doubted it was needed given the intensity of the look she leveled at me. "He needs a haven, a completely secure place, at least until he comes of age. Until he is eighteen."

I watched her for any flicker of surprise, any hesitation, but there was none. Her composure was absolute. I was confused by her composure. It was almost too serene, but I put it down to the lateness of the hour.

"His life might very well depend on quick, decisive action tonight," I continued, emphasizing the urgency as much as I could. "We've exhausted other options, and given the circumstances, this is the only place I could think of where he will be safe."

She listened, her gaze occasionally flickering to Angus before returning to me. When I finished, she gave a slow, deliberate nod.

"Thomas!" she commanded, her voice calm as it carried effortlessly into the dark orphanage. "Down here, please."

A short moment later, a boy, perhaps a year or two older than Angus, appeared at the top of the staircase, rubbing sleep from his eyes.

"Thomas, this is Angus," she instructed, her voice softening just a fraction for the still groggy boy. " He'll be staying with us. Take him upstairs and show him to the bed by the window, make sure he has everything he will need for the night." She looked at Angus, a hint of recognition flashing in her eyes. "Don't worry, Angus. Thomas will look after you for the night."

Angus straightened and silently turned his gaze on me as he gripped his blanket tighter. I nodded and gestured for him to follow Thomas. His shoulders shook with tears that shook me to my core. He turned and followed as Thomas led him away and up the dark staircase.

The woman then leveled her gaze back at me. "He will be safe, Detective. That much I can promise you."

Her words left no room for argument, a quiet certainty that did nothing to quell the uncertainty I felt.

"Now, as for you, Detective," she continued, her tone firm, making it clear that at least for tonight, my involvement with Angus was at an end. "I will need you to return tomorrow morning, first thing. Some procedures must be followed. Proper channels to go through to ensure that there are no issues with the legality of his time here."

I nodded, feeling oddly dismissed. She had taken control, as I had hoped she would, but her emotionless efficiency left me feeling off kilter. "Understood," and with that, I stepped back into the street. The heavy door clicked shut behind me.

As I walked away, I couldn't help but feel a sharp uncertainty, as if a rock had settled in the pit of my stomach. Each step left me feeling guiltier and guiltier.

When I returned early the next morning, I found Angus standing silently by the window. His eyes were fixed on the world outside, and the glass was thick with dust and cobwebs, as if neglect had taken over the place. His face was pale and almost ghostly, lit only by the faint glow of the first light creeping through the cracks. I could see the betrayal etched deep onto his features, as if he had been shattered from within without even realizing it. It was a look of pure hurt, caught between disappointment and shock, that made my chest tighten. My mind raced with questions—was it the experience, the loss, or something I had said or done? I couldn't shake the feeling that I was responsible for this change, that I had unintentionally carved this unnatural expression into his young face.

The sight of him like that struck me hard. I remembered how lively and full of hope he once looked, filled with dreams and innocence. Now, that hope seemed to have drained away, leaving behind only a hollow stare of abandonment. I knew I couldn't undo what was done. I hadn't yet found a way to comfort or reach him, and a part of me wondered if any words could bridge the gap that pain had created. For the moment, I saw no reason to take him away from that window or to disrupt the quiet brokenness that had settled over him. It felt like he needed

these moments of solitude, even if it hurt
me to see him like this. I understood,
somehow, that some wounds can't be seen or
healed with simple gestures. They linger
beneath the surface, shaping young faces
into masks of betrayal and sorrow.

Once I had finished signing all the
necessary papers to fully admit him into
Smyllum, which in the early morning light
looked more like an abandoned asylum than an
orphanage, I felt a strange chill run down
my spine. The room where I completed the
paperwork was cold and dimly lit. The air
seemed thick with dust and neglect. The
walls were cracked and stained, and the
faint smell of mildew hung heavily. I
couldn't help but notice how unwelcoming and
bleak the entire setting appeared. The staff
behind the desk, a woman with tired eyes and
a stiff manner, barely acknowledged me. Her
voice was flat and uninviting as she read
over the documents, barely glancing up.

Once I finally finished, I looked around for a way to see young Angus. I asked quietly, "Where is he?" expecting some gentle response or direction. Instead, her reaction was a loud, sharp whistle that echoed ominously through the hall. It was abrupt and startling, as if signaling a warning or an order in a prison. Without a word, she pointed sharply towards the staircase, then simply said, "He's upstairs." Her tone left no room for questions or conversation. She then turned her back and walked away as if I wasn't even there.

I was left to ascend the staircase and find him. The stairs were narrow, steep, and poorly maintained, stretching up through twelve flights. With each step, I could feel the weariness in my legs and the claustrophobic feeling growing stronger.

As I climbed, I took the opportunity to look around as much as I could, curious about the place I had just entered. I glimpsed rooms filled with broken furniture, peeling paint, and dark, empty corners. The hallway walls were lined with peeling wallpaper and faded posters, some torn and hanging loose. The flickering lights cast long, strange shadows on the old, scuffed floorboards. What I saw disturbed me more than I expected. The entire building exuded neglect and decay, with signs of disrepair everywhere. It was clear that no one cared enough to fix it up or keep it clean. I looked at the residents—if they could even be called that—and saw gaunt faces and restless eyes. The children's clothing was faded and torn. Some were sitting on battered chairs, others wandered without purpose. It was a stark contrast to any nurturing environment I imagined.

I couldn't shake the feeling that I had made a mistake signing those papers. The place was dirty, unorganized, and seemed more like a holding pen than a home. Looking around, I wished I had taken more time to

observe before committing and paying into
this so-called institution. My stomach
tightened with regret. I wondered what kind
of future awaited Angus here, in this
rundown, depressing place. Everything about
it made me feel uneasy. But now it was too
late. All I could do was continue ascending
those wiry stairs, hoping I'd find him safe
amid the chaos.

When I finally reached the top of the
stairs, I paused for a moment. I looked into
the room where Angus had been moved. What I
saw struck me immediately. The beds were so
close together, they almost looked like one
big dingy mattress stretched across the
floor. The room was small, cramped even,
with each bed pushed right up against the
next. The tight arrangement made the space
feel crowded, crowded with desperate pleas
and worry. The walls surrounding the beds
were painted a dull greenish-grey, like they
had been splashed with a tired, fading
color. The paint had lost its shine and

looked almost lifeless. Across the walls, I saw several chalkboard name tags taped or pinned, each one with a child's name written in shaky handwriting. The tags seemed like small signs of life, marks of identity in an otherwise plain room. These name tags told stories of children trying to stay connected, holding onto their identities amid uncertainty. The most striking sight, though, was something that stopped me cold. A familiar face, Thomas, the boy who brought Angus up here the night before, pointed to the bed by the window with an accusatory glare. In it sat Angus. His small figure looked tiny in the big room, but there was no mistaking him. He was peering out the window, still, his hand hovering over the dust on the sill. My throat tightened as I took in the symbols in the dust: ×ᛉ ᚠᛂᛠᛁᛂ ᛒᛂᚠᚠ ᚠᛂᚱ ᛁᛉᚾ, ᛈᛁᚾᛡ. ᛁᚠ ᛁ ᛏᛉᛉ×ᛏ, ᚠᛁᛂᛏ ᛠᛁ — ᛁ×ᚠᚠ ᛒᛁ ᚾᛂᛁᛏᛁᛂ.

They were so similar to the ones at the scene that I assumed Angus was the one who

drew them, and I thought them
inconsequential. My eyes locked on him
almost instinctively. It was like seeing a
piece of yesterday suddenly placed into
today's quiet chaos. The innocence in his
face, the same way he looked just a day
ago—small, vulnerable, and silent—carried a
heavy weight. All the details—the beds so
close, the gray dullness of the walls, the
chalkboard tags—faded into the background.
Only the boy remained, a sharp reminder of
the reason I was here. The reason I had come
so far, and the reason I couldn't look away.

The moment his eyes caught sight of me,
a wave of emotion spread across his face.
His eyes lit up with a bright, almost
desperate spark, as if hope had suddenly
broken through the clouds. Without
hesitation, he ran towards me, his steps
quick and eager. When he reached my side, he
threw his arms around me in a hug that was
tinged with sadness—tight but trembling, as
if he was holding onto something fragile. I

could feel his heart pounding through his small frame, and his soft, trembling voice reached me in a whisper that almost missed my ears. He begged me quietly, almost desperately, to take him away from that place, to save him from the uncertain future he faced there. His words were filled with a quiet plea, full of longing and fear, as he looked up at me with wide, pleading eyes that seemed too aged for his young face.

In that moment, I knew what I had to do. My mind was set, clear and firm. I simply could not stand the thought of leaving him behind, trapped in a situation that I knew was not safe or fair. It would be wrong to turn away, to ignore the silent cry for help coming from his tiny form. I gently loosened my arms around him, but I refused to let go completely. Instead, I gathered Angus carefully into my arms, cradling him as if holding something precious and fragile. As I did, I moved steadily toward the staircase that led down

into the foyer, feeling the weight of my
decision grow more resolved with each step.

When I reached the bottom of the
stairs, I saw the headmistress standing
there, her expression a mixture of concern
and curiosity. I knew I couldn't leave it to
chance that she would understand or agree.
So, I took a deep breath and stepped
forward. I asked her, firmly but politely,
to sign over legal guardianship of Angus to
me. I explained that he needed someone who
could watch over him constantly. Given the
number of children on the premises—over a
dozen at that time—staying vigilant was
impossible for her alone. There were too
many who could slip through the cracks or
get lost in the chaos. I told her that, with
me as his guardian, I could ensure he was
cared for properly, kept safe from harm, and
never left without someone watching over
him. My voice carried a quiet strength,
driven by a deep sense of responsibility and
love. I wanted her to understand that I was

ready to take on that role, no matter what
it took, because his safety depended on
someone like me.

ᚷᚤ ᚠᛣᚤᛁᛏ ᛒᛏᚱᚱ
ᚠᛣᚱ ᛁᛣᛘᛏᛘᚢ.
ᛁᚠ ᛁ ᚤᛋᛣᚷᚤ,
ᚠᛁᛋᛏᚤᛁ–ᛁᚷᚱᚱ
ᛒᛁ ᛘᛏᛁᛏᛏᛏ.

CASE FILE# 000004

CASE MANAGER: BRIANNA BAIRD

LEAD AGENT: GORDON McCurr

SUBJECT: Angus O'Connor

As we stepped into my home, Angus's face lit up with something pure; a simple—childish joy that couldn't be faked. His eyes sparkled with excitement, as if he had just discovered a new treasure. Even though he didn't say a word or make a sound, the way he looked at everything around him made me feel like I was the luckiest person alive. It was as if all the worries and stress of the day melted away in that moment. His small hands gripped mine tightly, as if trying to hold onto the happiness that was suddenly all around him. I could see the bright anticipation in his eyes, a look that told me he was dreaming of better things ahead, or maybe just a sense of comfort he had rarely felt before.

But that feeling, warm and full of promise, didn't last long. Just as quickly as his face had lit up, his expression changed. His shoulders sank, and tears started to form in his eyes. Without a word, he burst into quiet crying, his small body trembling as he struggled to hold back the tears. The sight of his distress hit me hard. I could tell from the way he sobbed softly that he was utterly exhausted. The day's events must have drained him completely. I knelt down and gently took his tiny hand in mine, feeling the slight shakes that still echoed his fatigue. I called him softly, trying to soothe him without adding pressure. Carefully, I guided him upstairs, each step slow but steady. We reached the room he'd be staying in during his visit, a small, cozy space filled with soft toys and a neatly made bed waiting for him. I rummaged through a drawer and grabbed a clean set of nightclothes that I knew he'd find comfortable—simple pajamas with a

cheerful pattern that I hoped would bring a
little comfort as he drifted off to sleep.

While he changed, I kept an eye on him,
watching as the worry and exhaustion melted
into a sleepy haze. When he finally crawled
into bed, I tucked the blankets around him
and sat quietly nearby. I turned off the
bedside lamp and let the room fall into
darkness, the soft glow from outside the
window illuminating a faint outline of his
face. I paused for a moment, wishing there
was something more I could do—something more
than just turning off the light or giving
him the blanket. I wondered if I could
somehow take away the fatigue that weighed
on him, or ease the sadness in his eyes. In
that quiet room, I thought about how much he
had gone through today, how children often
carry more than they can speak about. The
simple act of putting him to bed felt like a
small victory and a reminder of the
responsibility I had to make sure he felt
safe and cared for. I watched him for a few

seconds, trying to memorize the soft rise and fall of his chest, knowing the words I wanted to say would come later. For now, I just hoped the gentle darkness and the feeling of being close would help him find rest, even if I still wished I could do more for him.

It had only been a few hours since I had finally settled myself to sleep when suddenly I was pulled from my rest by an ear-shattering scream. The sound pierced through the quiet hall, coming from the room across from mine, and it made my heart race. For a moment, I lay frozen, trying to understand what I had just heard. My mind raced with fears of what might be happening to Angus. Without hesitation, I threw off the blankets and swung my legs over the side of the bed. Every muscle in my body felt tense as I hurried through the darkness, my mind jumping to worst-case scenarios—was he hurt? Was someone else in there with him?

As I reached his door, I hesitated for a second, my hand trembling as I grasped the doorknob. I told myself to stay calm, but my thoughts spun wildly. With a deep breath, I pushed the door open with force and stepped inside. The faint moonlight so often shining softly through the window was barely enough to reveal his small form thrashing on the bed. My eyes widened with both relief and horror, knowing instantly that he was in the grip of a terrible nightmare. His face was contorted, sweat glistening on his forehead, and his screams echoed from his throat. I felt a chill run down my spine as I watched him struggle, helpless to do anything more than try to soothe him.

Carefully, I reached out and gently shook his shoulder, trying not to startle him further. My hands were trembling just as much as I was inside, afraid of what might happen if I didn't act quickly. Slowly, his eyes darted open, unfocused and wide with terror, like he was seeing something

horrible no one else could. His screams
subsided into soft whimpers as he began to
wake, confusion flickering in his eyes. I
knew what he was going through wasn't
ordinary— nightmares often left children
trembling in their beds, but the intensity
of his distress seemed almost overwhelming.
I kept my touch soft, trying to ground him,
to remind him that it was just a nightmare
and that he was safe. It was moments like
these that reminded me how fragile a child's
mind can be, especially when shadowed by
fear or unsettling dreams. Angus's trembling
body and wide eyes told me he had seen
something terrifying, though he wouldn't
remember what once he woke fully, though to
my mortification there was a small part of
me that hoped to gain information from what
he had relived and that feeling battled with
the need to help relieve his terror.
Watching him settle down, I felt a knot
tighten in my stomach, knowing that whatever
had disturbed his sleep was enough to break

through the quiet hours of the night and send a ripple of fear through us all.

With everything that had happened in the boy's life, it was no surprise that he suffered from nightmares. After witnessing a murder, his mind was likely full of terrifying images and memories he could not shake. Is it common for children who see something so violent and unexpected to be haunted by dreams that replay the most frightening moments over and over? Then again, nightmares are a way for the mind to try to process trauma, but for someone so young, of course, they can be overwhelming. It must feel like a storm inside his head, pulling him into darkness.

Seeing a young boy afraid to sleep made my heart ache. It is a cruel twist of fate that someone so innocent has to face such intense fear. A child's world should be filled with wonder, not with

images of violence that shake his sense
of safety. It's hard to picture the
kind of terror he must have felt,
waking up unsure if the danger was
truly gone. As the night continued so
too did the nightmares. It took Angus
ten long minutes to settle down after
one of these episodes. He would lie
trembling, eyes wide open, caught in a
state between the unconscious state of
fear and the security of his reality. I
watched him struggle in the throes of
pain that made breathing seem
difficult. The worry that haunted me
was not just about his sleepless night,
but about the fear holding him back
from closing his eyes and finding
peace, which would allow me to discern
the truth of what really happened that
night. By 2:00 a.m. Angus was afraid to
fall asleep again, the idea of slipping
into darkness seemed more frightening

than facing his fears during waking hours.

The rest of the early morning passed quietly. No strange noises broke the silence, and the darkness stayed still and unchanging. I finally drifted into a deep sleep and woke just before I heard a sudden, unexpected thunder rumble. It was a low, powerful sound that made the whole room shake slightly. Light flashes lit up the sky outside—bright, quick bursts of lightning that flickered through the window. The storm seemed to have come out of nowhere, catching me off guard. When I sat up, I knew it was time to wake Angus. He had slept peacefully for the remainder of the night— or so I thought. I was surprised to find that he was already awake and dressed. He sat on the edge of his bed in clean clothes, looking calm, as if he had been expecting me to wake soon. It

struck me how unusual that was, given
how restless the night had been for the
both of us.

As I looked at him, a sudden thought
crossed my mind. He looked a little more
alert than I was expecting, and some small
signs of hunger started to dawn on me. It
was nothing I could see outright—no obvious
signs of breakfast or snacks—but that faint
feeling in my stomach, that gnawing
emptiness, made me suspicious. My intuition
told me he might be hungry, even if he
hadn't said anything yet. Before I could
even say a word, I heard it: a soft, low
rumbling sound from his stomach. It was like
a gentle growl, barely noticeable but loud
enough in the quiet room. The noise seemed
to confirm my guess—he was indeed hungry.
The strange part was how he reacted to this.
Instead of trying to hide it, his cheeks
flushed a little, and his eyes darted away
shyly. It was almost as if he was
apologizing for feeling hungry, like it was

a mistake he shouldn't have made— a small sign of vulnerability.

It tugged at my heart to see him react that way, like he was trying to shrink into himself, afraid of being a burden or showing weakness. That moment made me realize how much little things can reveal about a person. His quiet shame, his effort to hide his hunger—these tiny signals showed me how much he might be hiding. I could feel a tight squeeze in my chest at the sight of him. Once again I was in a quandary, I need to know the truth. It was hard to see someone so small, so careful with their feelings, while simply being hungry. It made me think about all the times we often hide our needs and hopes, even from ourselves... His shy glance and reddening face told me that he wasn't just hungry—he was also a little worried about how I would react or what I might think. That single, vulnerable moment exposed a quiet fear that maybe, just maybe...

"BY MY SHILLELAGH! Whit am A doin
sittin here contemplatin life while this wee
lad is starvin tae death!"

After hurriedly finishing my breakfast,
I knew I had to hurry back to the evidence I
collected. Leaving Angus at the kitchen
table I spread out the items on a clean
surface in my study. Focusing on the small
pieces of material I found beneath Iris's
nails, it became clear to me that these tiny
fragments could be important. They appeared
to be bits of skin, perhaps scraped off
during a struggle or even from contact with
the scoundrel. I carefully examined each
piece under a bright light, hoping to find
something more useful. My main intention was
to find traces of DNA—deoxyribonucleic
acid—that could tie someone to the crime
scene or the victim.

If I had a proper lab setup or advanced
testing tools, I could analyze the skin

cells for DNA. DNA is like a unique fingerprint for each person. It can identify who was at the scene, what they touched, or who they battled with. The problem was that I didn't have access to the kind of equipment that can pull DNA out of a tiny skin sample. That kind of testing needs specialized labs, expensive machines, and skilled technicians. Without that, the tiny bits of skin wouldn't tell me anything useful. They'd just be small tidbits of indecipherable clues without any way to connect them to a specific person. It was frustrating. I knew that if I had a way to analyze the DNA, this evidence could be a game-changer. It might confirm a suspect's identity, link them to the scene, or even help clear someone if they weren't involved. But right now, the reality was different. There was no quick or simple way I could test those skin fragments for genetic material. That evidence was essentially useless, it was not enough to lead to a conclusion, and that left me with a missing puzzle piece and a growing sense of disappointment.

As Angus finished eating his breakfast, I suddenly realized that leaving him all alone probably wasn't the best idea. Children need to be around others, especially when they're adjusting to new environments. He was still young, still growing. It was clear that staying at home wouldn't give him the kind of support he needed to feel safe, cared for, and maybe even a bit more confident.

I thought about how children often open up more when they are in the presence of others they trust. Angus is a child, after all, and children tend to be more comfortable around people they see as friends or mentors. I knew that if he came with me to the headquarters, he might loosen up and share more about what he's feeling or thinking. Being around my colleagues— whom I refer to as my "fellow gumshoes" —would probably help him feel less intimidated and more at ease. They're people who've worked with me long enough to understand how to talk to kids, and I believe they'd be able to connect with him better than I could alone.

CASE FILE# 000005

CASE MANAGER: BRIANNA BAIRD

LEAD AGENT: GORDON McCurr

SUBJECT: Angus O'Connor

It only took a few minutes of walking to reach the station. As I approached, my mind was racing with thoughts about Iris and the strange lead I had just been handed. It seemed like a small clue, but in the world of crime and secrets, even the tiniest detail can open a new door. The man who lived nearby had seen something that might be connected to her murder. A few days ago, he had noticed someone lurking around the same area—someone who seemed out of place— suspicious. I tried to picture what that moment must have looked like: a shadowy figure, hiding behind a tree or maybe walking quickly past a dark alley. Whatever it was, the man's statement could be the piece of the puzzle I needed.

I turned my gaze to the young boy standing beside me. He had been quiet, but I knew he had listened carefully. For the first time, I really looked at him and felt a strange twist in my chest. Initially, I had brought him along as part of my investigation— but now I could see I was growing attached to him. I often wondered what it might feel like to be a real father—what it would be like to watch someone grow, learn, and face the world with true support. Now, after just a few hours of caring for him, I knew the answer. The bond had formed so quickly, so strongly, that there was no backing away. I couldn't imagine a life without this feeling— not now that I'd experienced the sense of responsibility and connection that came with looking after someone so entirely. The thought made me realize how much my perspective had shifted in such a short time and how much more life this young boy was beginning to give me.

When we arrived back at the station, I explained to him that I needed to leave him there for a while, reminding him that he would be safe, and that I had a lead to follow. I didn't think it was safe for him to make the journey with me.

I also made sure to explain clearly that he would be staying with Mrs. Bishop, the woman who handled the phones at the station during this time. In addition, I wanted her to understand everything about what he was going through so she could help take care of him properly. I felt a bit uneasy about leaving him with her, even though I knew she was kind and caring. Still, I worried about whether she could fully understand the depth of his struggles and how sensitive he was to certain triggers. But I reminded myself that Mrs. Bishop and he had met before and that, as a mother herself, I believed she would keep a

watchful eye on him and be gentle but firm
in helping him feel safe. I also knew she
had dealt with children who had their own
challenges before, so she would be patient
and attentive.

Once I was sure he understood, I
crouched down to his level, and gave him a
tight, comforting hug. I wrapped my arms
around him tightly because I knew hugs could
help calm his nerves. I looked into his eyes
and told him I cared for him very much and
that I would not be gone long. My voice was
soft but steady, trying to lend him
strength. After the hug, I gently brushed a
hand through his hair and gave him a little
smile to reassure him. I stood up, slowly,
took a final deep breath, and made my way
towards the door. I knew it was important to
leave him with someone he could trust, but I
also couldn't ignore the trepidation that
still tugged at me.

As I stepped out into the cool air, I
turned my attention to the station's buggy,

its worn wooden frame was creaking softly as I approached. My focus shifted then to the house of Mr. McCarter, a man who might hold vital clues that could help us find Iris' killer. His house was small but neat, sitting quietly on the edge of town with a worn front porch and a garden overgrown with weeds. I pushed open the gate, tried to clear my mind, and headed straight for his door. I raised my hand to knock, but as my fist made contact with the solid wood, the door unexpectedly swung inward. It didn't creak nor shut behind me; instead, it swung open smoothly. A sharp, coppery smell rushed into my nostrils, instantly recognizable. My stomach tightened as I inhaled. That scent was blood—a smell I was all too familiar with. most of my work involved homicide. I shuddered involuntarily, the image of violent death flashing in my mind. Without hesitation, I pushed the door open farther and stepped inside. The air was thick, heavy with that unmistakable metallic odor, and I braced myself to face whatever truth this house might reveal. Every step I took was deliberate, each movement guided by a mix of professional instinct and quiet dread. The house felt silent but charged with a dark energy that told me I wouldn't find peace here easily. I knew this was a place where secrets hid behind every corner, waiting to be uncovered.

As I stepped into the hallway, an unsettling feeling hit me suddenly, twisting in my stomach. My instincts screamed that something was terribly wrong. I called out for Mr. McCarter, hoping he would answer and reassure me, but my voice was met with silence—no response. I hesitated for a moment, then took a few more cautious steps forward, my eyes darting around in search of any sign of life or trouble. I peeked around the corner into the kitchen, my heart pounding faster as the shock hit me hard. What I saw there made my blood run cold, my mind racing to process the sight before me.

The only lead we had managed to find
earlier suddenly felt meaningless. It was
now clear that the situation was far more
serious than I had imagined. There, in the
shadows of the kitchen, I discovered a
second body in as many days—a stark contrast
to the quiet house I had entered. He was
leaning against the wall, stiff and
unmoving. His skin was cold to the touch, as
if he had been dead for hours, not minutes.
His face looked peaceful yet distant, as if
time had frozen him in place. The stark
stillness sent a shiver down my spine. I
took a quick scan of the surroundings,
trying to spot anything that could point to
the murder weapon or reveal what had
happened. The room was silent but tense,
filled with the weight of this cruel
discovery. The only thing out of place was a
faint smell of blood lingering in the air.
As I moved closer to examine him, my eyes
caught a glimpse of the backyard through the
kitchen window. Outside, lying in a small

puddle of muddy water, was a blood-stained fire poker. The metal glinted sickly in the dim light, its battered handle soaked with crimson. The sight of it made the hair on my arms stand up, hinting that this was likely the murder weapon. The bloody poker seemed abandoned outside, as if whoever wielded it had rushed away, leaving behind a trail of violence. My mind raced to piece everything together—the cold body, the blood-stained weapon, the quiet, foreboding atmosphere—each detail pulling me deeper into the dark truth that lay behind this horrifying scene.

I moved carefully across the room toward the new rotary telephone sitting on the side table. My hands felt steady despite the situation. I picked up the receiver and pressed it to my ear. I dialed the station's number, knowing it was my job, as a detective, to report what I'd found. My voice sounded calm, even firm, as I described everything I had stumbled upon. I told the station master about walking into Mr. McCarter's home and finding his body cold and still in the kitchen. I explained how the room was quiet except for the faint hum of the gas lights and the ticking of the clock. I described the scene in detail—how the body looked, the position it was in, and the slight stench that told me he had died recently. I also mentioned that there appeared to be no sign of forced entry or a struggle aside from the obvious blunt force trauma and identified the firepoker as the murder weapon, which indicated foul play. After I finished explaining, the station master listened carefully and assured me that he would send some Constables right away. He told me they would take the body to the morgue and then get my official statement. I felt a small sense of relief knowing help was on the way, but I still had to wait. I leaned against the wall and looked at my watch. Time stretched slowly. About forty-five minutes to an hour went by.

The house grew quiet again, except for the occasional distant bells and muffled voices outside. My stomach felt tight, but I kept my eyes on the clock, waiting for the Constables to arrive.

Finally, the door swung open, and four constables in uniform stepped inside. They moved with purpose and precision. I stepped aside to let them in, then led the way to the kitchen. I carefully pushed the door open, revealing the scene I'd described over the phone. The men huddled close, taking in every detail. One constable pulled out a notebook and started taking notes. Another examined the body carefully, glancing at the position of the limbs and the expression on Mr. McCarter's face. The third constable asked a few questions, scribbling answers in his notebook. The last one quickly checked the room for anything unusual—scattered papers, a broken glass, or anything that could be a clue.

We spent the next three hours going
over everything carefully— a standard time
for this type of investigation. I told them
step-by-step what I had seen, from the
moment I entered the house, to finding Mr.
McCarter on the kitchen floor, to the small
details I noticed—like the slightly open
cabinet door and the half-finished cup of
tea on the table. I answered questions about
the time of death, possible motives, and
anything suspicious I might have noticed
earlier. They took notes, asked for
clarification, and seemed focused on
gathering every fact. It was a slow,
detailed process, but I knew this was
crucial. After answering their questions and
providing all the details I could, I felt
confident I had done my part. It was late,
and I was exhausted. The Constables gathered
their gear, exchanged a few words, and left
the house. I was left alone in the quiet
room, knowing I'd done what I could. I made
my way back to the station, walking through

the dark streets, and finally, after all the effort, I arrived back, ready to give my official statement and see the case move forward.

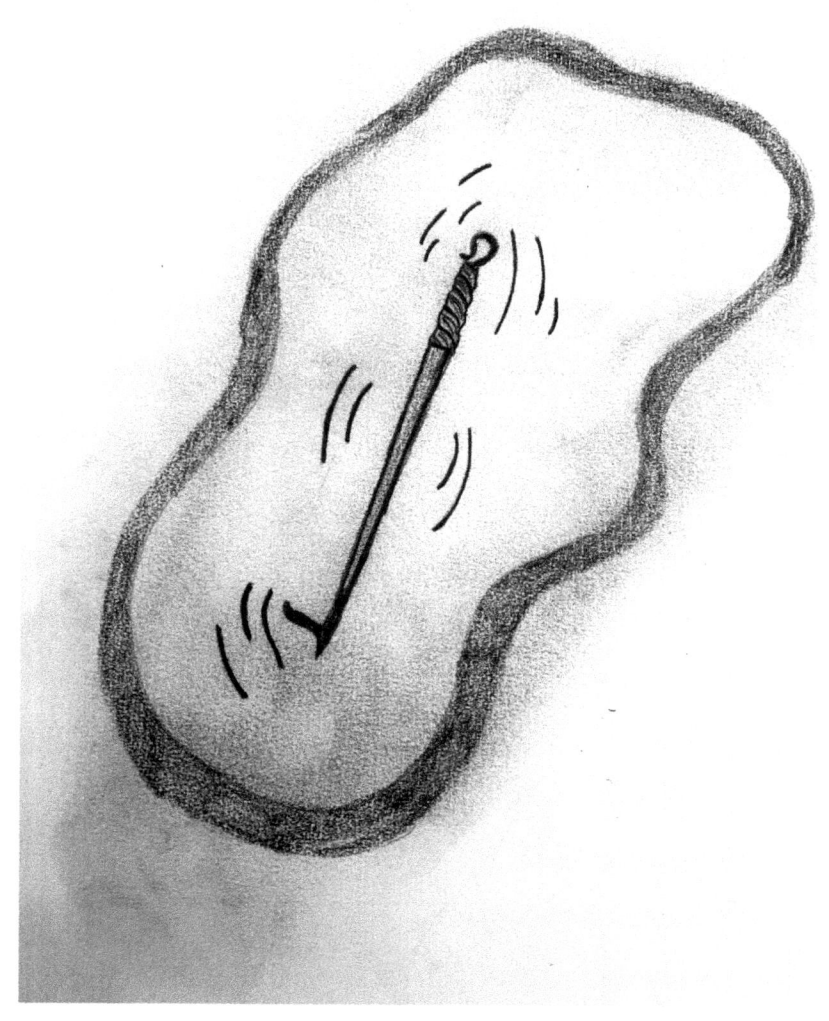

CASE FILE# 000006

CASE MANAGER: BRIANNA BAIRD

LEAD AGENT: GORDON McCurr

SUBJECT: Angus O'Connor

As I stepped into the station, a sudden wave of relief swept over me, and I let out a breath I hadn't realized I was holding. My eyes immediately found Angus sitting at my desk, calmly munching on an apple. He was completely at ease, reading a piece of paper that was resting on top of a cluttered pile. Despite the tragic loss of his mother just a few days ago, he carried a small, light smile on his face. That simple expression seemed to defy the chaos around us, showing a quiet resilience that I couldn't help but notice. Still young and innocent, he radiated a carefree innocence that felt out of place in such a dark time. I couldn't help but chuckle softly when his face suddenly scrunched up in confusion and curiosity, eyes narrowing as he tried to understand whatever had just caught his attention. That goofy, puzzled look on his face broke the silence and made me laugh loud enough for him to turn his head toward me so quickly. His eyes widened with shock at my sudden laughter, and for a moment, he looked unsure of what to do. Then, just as fast, that shock melted into a bright, weighted happiness. Without hesitation, he shot across the room, ran straight to me, and threw his small arms around my waist, hugging me tight. He fit perfectly in that moment, belonging there, safe and loved despite the chaos that had touched his life. His attention turned back to the paper. I glanced down and realized it was a report I needed to review closely before sending it upstairs.

The report detailed the particulars of the latest theft in the city—an armed robbery that had left the neighborhood shaken, an armed robber had burst into a jeweler's shop on the Royal Mile, just as

the evening fog rolled in thick from the
Firth of Forth. He waved a pistol at the
shopkeeper and two customers, demanding gold
watches and silver chains with a snarl that
echoed through the narrow close. The man
fired a warning shot into the ceiling,
splintering plaster and sending folks
scrambling for cover. Jewels scattered
across the wooden floor like spilled stars.
He grabbed a fistful of valuables—enough to
fund a life on the run, I reckoned—and
vanished into the misty alleys before the
bobbies could respond. The neighborhood
buzzed with fear that night. Folks bolted
their doors early, whispering about shadows
in the wynds. Shop owners boarded windows,
and mothers kept children indoors by the
hearth. This robbery shook us all, a bold
strike right in the heart of old Edinburgh,
where trust once walked hand in hand with
the cobbled paths. I traced the words again,
noting the robber's height from witness
sketches—tall, cloaked in a dark

greatcoat—and the direction he fled toward the Canongate. Such crimes had risen in our growing city, with the poor crowding in from the countryside and tempting fates in the shadows. But this one cut deep, leaving scars on the honest folk who built these tenements stone by stone. I was tasked with making sure everything was correct, catching any mistakes that could slow down the investigation. In this quiet moment, I wondered how much a child like Angus could really understand about all this chaos. My focus shifted back to the report, but part of me kept looking at Angus, grateful for the brief moment of normalcy he brought. I promised myself I would do everything I could to protect it.

Even though it was only a little past one in the afternoon, I felt a wave of exhaustion hit me hard. The day had taken so many unexpected turns—things I never saw coming. As I watched Angus, I couldn't help but notice how much he resembled his father.

Their features—those deep-set eyes and that gentle curve of his nose—made it almost like a photograph. It stirred a quiet sadness in me. The thought that this boy had never truly known his father sank deep. His father had disappeared from his life when he was just barely four. He hadn't had the chance to grow up knowing him, understand him, or even see his smile. All he had were vague stories, faint memories, and maybe some old photographs that didn't quite capture who his father really was. The mystery of Mr. O'Connor's disappearance haunted me for years. It stuck in my thoughts like a shadow that would not fade. His father had been a top muckraker back in the day. That meant he was an investigative reporter who dug deep into scandals and corruption. Then one day he just disappeared, no note, no clue as to where to start searching for him. That left me and a team of detectives scratching our heads. We chased every lead, but they all went cold. No fingerprints. No witnesses who

saw a thing. The empty trail mocked our
efforts. Frustration built up fast. We spent
long nights poring over files that led
nowhere. It felt like the case slipped
through our fingers every time. Now, as I
look back, those months stand out as a
whirlwind of work. Cases poured in like rain
during a storm. There were bold thefts from
local shops and banks. People reported items
gone in the blink of an eye. Then came more
disappearances, just like O'Connor's father.
Folks vanished from their homes or streets,
leaving families in panic. We also dealt
with hints of organized crime pulling
strings behind it all. Gangs seemed to link
these events, with whispers of threats and
hidden deals. Yet, no matter how hard we
pieced it together, nothing tied back to
O'Connor's case. It stayed isolated, a
puzzle with missing parts that drove us mad.
Perhaps one day I will find a connection.

It broke my heart because I knew how
children need their parents to grow strong

and confident. They need their stories, their lessons, their love. Now, this boy's face was a reminder of what could have been—a life with stories and memories that were never made. As I sat there, deep in these thoughts, it suddenly hit me like a sharp jolt. His mother had died just three days ago, and yet, something about her case felt similar to his father's disappearance. I realized I hadn't put together the pieces before—how her death might be connected to his father's absence. Maybe they both left suddenly, tragically, in ways that left behind more questions than answers. Either way, it made everything seem even heavier. I asked myself how often we get so caught up in what's immediate that we forget to see the bigger picture. I couldn't shake the feeling that in some way, these tragedies were connected. That somehow, beneath all the pain, there was a story waiting to be uncovered, a story that might someday explain it all.

I carried young Angus back to my house and then spent a lot of time mentally organizing everything I knew about his mothers's murder and his father's sudden disappearance. At first, nothing seemed out of place or gave me any clear clues. Nothing jumped out as suspicious. I just kept piling up facts, details, and small bits of information, hoping something would click. I stood before the cork board I'd nailed to the wall. It started as a simple map of the city streets, but now it groaned under the weight of scribbled notes, yellowed newspaper clippings, and faded photographs pinned in frantic clusters. Iris's death haunted me most—shot clean through the chest in her own entryway on Kenmure Ave…I tacked up every scrap of the report from Angus's memory of the night to the Coroners report on the path of the bullet. Across the board, strings of red yarn stretched to Mr. McCarter's case, that brutal end in his cramped kitchen off the same streed. Fire poker to the skull. I added timelines side by side, marking the hours: Iris at dusk on a Tuesday, McCarter just after dawn two days later. Locations overlapped too close—both homes mere houses apart in the Old Town's twisty lanes. I stepped back, rubbing my temples, fingers ink-stained from hours of jotting. Nothing linked solid yet, no smoking gun or clear motive to tie the killer's hand. But I kept at it, pinning one more detail, one more thread, praying the chaos would snap into focus and reveal the fiend who struck twice in our shadowed city. It was like trying to piece together a puzzle with missing pieces—frustrating but necessary. Then, when I added in the most recent murder, the pieces started aligning in strange ways. Small details I hadn't noticed before suddenly caught my attention. They all pointed back to Angus in some way. It was like the more I looked, the more I saw connections forming around him.

I decided to dig deeper into the
background of Mr. McCarter, who had been
involved with Angus's life in a seemingly
innocent way. I learned that Mr. McCarter
often watched over Angus when Iris was busy
working. On many afternoons, he'd be there
in the background, keeping an eye on a young
boy whose life was wrapped in quiet
routines. I wondered what an innocent kid
like Angus could possibly have to do with
two brutal murders and a mysterious
disappearance. It didn't make sense at
first. How could a child be involved in
something so dark? The thought lingered in
my mind, stirring up more questions. Was it
possible that Angus had witnessed something
that I didn't see? Or maybe he was somehow
connected?

I kept asking myself why Mr. McCarter, a
seemingly normal man who watched after a
young boy, would be involved or linked to
all this violence. His role seemed small,
almost harmless, yet I couldn't shake the

feeling that there was more to his presence than met the eye. That he watched Angus so often made me wonder if he knew something or if he was guarding him for a darker reason. As I sifted through every detail, I couldn't ignore the growing pattern. Every new piece of information pointed in the same direction. Angus, the boy who looked so innocent, might hold the key to understanding what really happened.

Questions flooded my mind. I remembered stories about children who saw too much, children whose quiet observations unveiled secrets adults tried to hide. Was Angus one of them? Why else would so many tiny clues seem to orbit around him? It seemed strange that among all the people involved, his name kept popping up in my thoughts. My mind was flooded with possibilities, yet I couldn't ignore the growing sense that this innocent-seeming child might have been at the center of something much darker than anyone suspected. I wondered how I could

have been so blind to even entertain that
notion.

It was clear to me now that I must have
been losing my mind to think there was some
kind of personal vendetta aimed directly at
the O'Connor family. No, that idea couldn't
be true. It made no sense—nothing about it
added up, and yet a tiny voice inside warned
me that I couldn't dismiss it entirely. I
knew I needed to stay calm, but that was
easier said than done.

Later that evening, just as darkness
settled in, a fierce thunderstorm rolled in
unexpectedly. The sky darkened rapidly, and
the wind picked up strength, shaking the
house with its loud howls. Each time thunder
roared across the sky, it was as if a
gunshot had gone off, sharp and sudden. The
deep booms echoed through the night like
distant explosions, making my heart race.
For some reason, the sound of the thunder
hit me differently that night. It sounded
just like gunfire—like shots fired in quick

succession. That realization hit me like a punch to the stomach. My pulse quickened, and I felt a wave of panic rising inside. Without thinking, I bolted from my room, rushing down the hall in search of Angus. I needed to make sure he was safe. When I entered his room, I paused in horror. His bed was a mess of rumpled sheets, but more disturbing was that he was gone. His blanket was tossed aside, and there was no sign of him anywhere. My breath caught in my throat, and I felt a surge of fear swallow me whole. My mind raced with questions. Had he left? Was he hurt? Or worse? I couldn't stop myself from panicking as I stared around the empty space where he should have been.

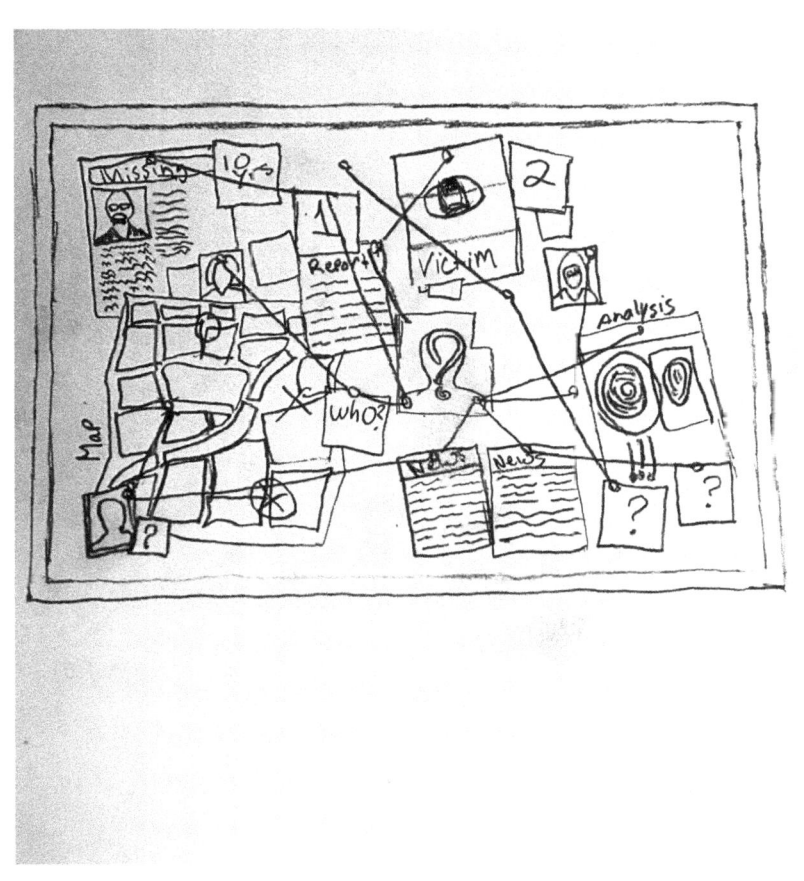

CASE FILE # 000007

CASE MANAGER: BRIANNA BAIRD

LEAD AGENT: GORDON McCurr

SUBJECT: Angus O'Connor

My thoughts spun wildly with a flood of
possibilities as I desperately tore through
closets and shoved aside dusty blankets
under beds. Every space I checked felt like
a race against time, a frantic attempt to
find Angus before something happened. He was
nowhere to be found, vanished into thin air.
Worry gnawed at my mind like a relentless
beast. I called out his name again and again
as I searched each room, but no sign of him.
The house was eerily quiet except for my
frantic footsteps and swallowed breaths. My
heart pounded harder with each passing
minute, growing heavier with fear that I
might never find him. I kept replaying all
the places he might have gone. Maybe he
headed to headquarters? Could he have
visited his house? I imagined him wandering

through streets, lost or maybe in trouble. I
wondered what I would do if I found him and
discovered that something had triggered
flashbacks or painful memories. Yet, could
those memories be the key I need to unlock
the treasure trove of answers or Pandora's
Box. That thought made my stomach tighten.

Outside, dark clouds gathered overhead,
and suddenly a heavy downpour burst from the
sky, drenching everything in a matter of
seconds. The rain was relentless, pounding
against the roof and splattering on the
cobbles. I didn't hesitate; I had to leave
immediately. As I dashed out the door, I
realized I had forgotten to lock it. For a
brief moment, I considered turning back,
knowing that leaving the house unsecured
wasn't wise. Urgency forced me to press on,
ignoring the small voice of doubt telling me
to be cautious.

The walk to Angus's house took about
twenty minutes it seemed painfully slow,
with each step soaked in rain and growing

more dire. The savage wind bit into my rain soaked my clothes, leaving them cold and heavy, seeping into my skin. The streets were nearly empty, only the distant rumble of thunder in the background. My mind kept racing, imagining all the terrible things that might happen if I didn't find him soon. Was he cold and scared somewhere? Had he wandered into danger, or had the target been… My grip tightened on the small gun I held tightly, my eyes scanning every shadow and corner of the neighborhood. When I finally reached his house, I pushed open the front gate and hurried inside.

I had searched the entire house for what felt like forever, but in reality it was only ten minutes. He was curled up tightly in the same corner where we had discovered him the night of the murder. The room was dim, shadows creeping along the walls as if the darkness was trying to hide what had happened here. His small frame trembled, shivering uncontrollably as if the cold had seeped right into his bones. I looked down at the boy's face and saw his eyes glazed with fear and shock. Tears streamed silently down his cheeks, leaving streaks on his pale face, and for a moment, I was frozen by a wave of emotion.

I gently knelt beside him, feeling the uneven heartbeat pounding in his tiny chest. Carefully, I pulled him into my arms, trying to offer some comfort amid the chaos around us. But as I held him close, I was surprised at how cold he was—his small hands and face barely warm to my touch. Was it the result of his escape through the elements… or— what had just occurred. Without wasting a second, I slowly stood up, taking him carefully in my arms, and made my way upstairs, which was quiet and eerily still.

Inside his room, chaos still lingered. A few belongings were scattered across the floor—his favorite toy, a book left open—all items that had been forgotten in the rush and panic of the crime scene. It was clear that in the chaos of the night, everything he cared about had been jumbled and left behind. The air in the room carried a heavy silence, broken only by his shallow breathing and the faint crackle of an old ceiling fan overhead. Every item on the floor told a story of hurried steps and pandemonium. His pajamas crumpled on the bed, a picture frame laying face down, glass shattered on the carpet… I looked around at this small space, wondering what he had been doing when this nightmare began, what had he seen, or what memories clung to this room connecting the terrible event that changed everything. As I wrapped him in a warm blanket I found nearby, I realized the coldness I felt wasn't just physical. It matched the chill inside me—a mixture of fear and helplessness that refused to fade.

CASE FILE#000008

CASE MANAGER: BRIANNA BAIRD

LEAD AGENT: GORDON McCurr

SUBJECT: Angus O'Connor

The walk back home felt endless. Every step seemed heavier than the last, and my legs burned from the long, exhausting journey. The sky was losing daylight, casting shadows that stretched across the street and made everything seem more ominous. By the time we arrived at the door, I couldn't shake the feeling that something was wrong. My eyes fell on a small, fragile slip of paper wedged into the narrow gap between the door and the wall. It looked like someone had slipped it there deliberately, hiding it just out of plain sight. The note was brief, but it carried a weight that made my stomach tighten. I reached out carefully and pulled it free, unfolding the thin paper with trembling fingers.

Once inside, I looked at Angus. His clothes were soaked through, heavy with rain, and he looked up at me with wide, frightened eyes. I gently guided him inside, making sure he was safe from the cold and damp. "Go upstairs and change into dry clothes," I told him softly. "Your clothes are soaked and I don't want you to catch cold." He nodded without a word and started up the stairs slowly, each step revealing his troubled mind.

While he headed upstairs, I took a moment to examine the note that had been slipped inside. I felt my stomach tighten as I read the words. The message was small, but the threat it carried was loud and clear. It said, "***I KNOW WHERE ANGUS IS AND HE IS NEXT...***". on the bottom of the note were familiar symbols, though I could not remember at the moment why they were familiar: ᛁ ᚲᚾᛟᚹ ᛁᛟᚢ ᚲᚨᚾ ᚱᛖᛞ ᚦᛁᛊ, ᚨᛜᚢᛊ. ᛁᚷᛗ ᛏᚱᛁᛁᛜ ᛏᛟ ᛈᚱᛟᛏᛖᚲᛏ ᛁᛟᚢ. ᚹᚺᛁ ᚹᛟᚾᚷᛏ ᛁᛟᚢ ᛚᛖᛏ ᛗᛖ.

The words I could understand seemed to jump off the paper, even though they were written in simple handwriting. A cold chill ran down my spine. Someone knew where Angus was, and they wanted him. The note made it crystal clear—he was a target. The idea that someone was watching us, waiting to strike, filled me with dread. It was the kind of danger I rarely encountered in my life—the unpredictable, ruthless threat.

In that moment, I couldn't shake the feeling that if I let him out of my sight, something terrible might happen. I had to be extra cautious. Whoever this person was, they weren't playing games or taking chances. They had plans—plans that involved Angus. I knew I had to keep him close, keep him safe, even if it meant staying awake all night and watching every door. The stakes had just gotten much higher. Angus, still trembling from the shock of recent events, was suddenly in the middle of something dangerous, something I couldn't fathom. And

I realized that I would do whatever it took to keep him out of harm's way, no matter the cost.

I saw Angus slowly walking down the stairs, his face tired and shadows darkening his eyes. He moved with sluggish steps. My heart quickened, and I hurried to slip the threatening note into my pocket before he could notice. I knew I had to hide it carefully, to keep my plan safe from his watchful gaze. As soon as Angus finally reached the bottom of the staircase, he made a beeline for the study door. Without hesitation, he climbed onto my lap—his small frame curling into me in a quiet plea for comfort. Almost instantly, his eyelids fluttered shut, and he began to drift off into a world of dreams. His breathing softened, and I could see the faint rise and fall of his chest as he entered that peaceful sleep. There was a flicker of hope in my mind that he might rest soundly throughout the night, free from worries or pain. It was a small hope, but a hope I clung to tightly.

Carefully, I lifted him from my lap and carried him up the stairs. Each step felt heavier than the last, weighed down by the burden of carrying his fragile, tired body. I gently laid him on the bed and pulled the thick blankets up to his chin, needing to shield him from the world. I frowned as I watched him shiver beneath the two heavy blankets—his tiny frame trembling despite the warmth they offered. His small hands curled tightly against his chest as if trying to warm himself. I leaned over him and placed the back of my hand on his forehead, gently checking his temperature. I was startled by the heat radiating from his skin, a clear sign that his fever was worsening. It made my stomach tighten with concern—this wasn't just exhaustion.

His brow crinkled in a restless, feverish line, and I saw the nightmarish confusion flicker behind his closed eyes. That look scared me; it showed how much the fever was affecting him. My mind quickly raced with what to do. I hurried down the stairs, trying to steady my breath as anxiety filled me, and grabbed a handful of dry kindling along with several logs of wood. I needed enough wood to keep the fire burning through the night, to keep him warm and possibly help bring down his fever. Carrying the wood was harder than usual; my pace slowed as I struggled with the weight of the logs. My arms ached, but I knew I had to get them up there, fast. Every step was deliberate, each movement purposeful, driven by a need. The house was quiet except for the faint crackling of the fire waiting for me upstairs, a small comfort in the dead of the night.

When I stepped into Angus's room, a shiver ran down my back. It felt like the air suddenly grew colder, as if the temperature had dropped several degrees just a moment before, like death was lurking in the shadows. The dim light revealed the chaos of the scene: Angus was tangled tightly in his blankets, his small frame twitching with each shudder. His face was flushed red, lips dry and cracked, and beads of sweat clung to his forehead. His breathing was shallow, and faint murmurs escaped his lips, barely audible but filled with discomfort. The room seemed to echo with his restless wheezing, creating an unsettling quiet that hung heavy in the air. The reality was harsh—his body was too drained for action. This feeling of helplessness pressed down hard, mixing worry with desperation as I stood there, unsure of how to make him better or how long he could hold on without proper help.

ᛁ ᚲᛟᚹ ᛁᛟᚢ ᚲᚠᚷ
ᚱᛗᛟᚦᛁᛖ ᚠᛟᚾᛖ,
ᛁᚷᚨ ᛏᚱᛁᛟ ᛏᛟ
ᛚᚱᛟᛏᛗᚲᛏ ᛁᛟᚢ.
ᚹᚺᛁ ᚹᛟᛏᛏ ᛁᛟᚢ
ᛚᛖᛏ ᚨᚨᛖ.

CASE FILE# 000009

CASE MANAGER: BRIANNA BAIRD

LEAD AGENT: GORDON McCurr

SUBJECT: Angus O'Connor

I hurried down the hallway and darted into my room without hesitation. My fingers trembled slightly as I grabbed my phone to call the O'Connor's family doctor. I pressed the numbers quickly, and waited anxiously for the line to connect. Every time the phone rang, my patience wore thin. The repetitive sound of the ringing grew more irritating with each ring.

Suddenly, the ringing stopped, leaving only a deafening silence. I clenched my jaw as I stared at the silent phone. Then, a tired voice finally answered. It sounded exhausted, as if he'd just finished a long shift or hadn't slept in days. I didn't waste a second. Without polite greetings, I explained the situation—how Angus was burning up, his skin was hot to the touch,

and he kept moaning in restless sleep. The
doctor listened quietly and then assured me
he would be arriving soon. He promised he'd
be at my house within the next fifteen
minutes. I clutched the phone tightly, with
both relief and dread. I kept checking
Angus, who was lying in his bed. His face
was flushed, and he kept whispering or
mumbling in his sleep. For a brief moment it
seemed as if he were reliving the night of
the crime. If only I could decipher… the
groan sounded as if he said "Mr. Mc
Car"..and then his voice trailed off. In
between the staccato beat of his fingers
tapping that repeating pattern on the
blanket there seemed to be a murmur of
"mum?"

Every few seconds, his breathing seemed
labored, and I could see the sweat beading
on his forehead. I knelt beside the worn
armchair, the cool floorboards pressing
against my knees, but I barely noticed the
discomfort. My hands were clasped so tightly

my knuckles were white. "Please,God, I know that you are merciful. Hasn't he been through enough? God, I understand that you are almighty and according to your Word, in Romans, 8, I think 28, you said 'we know that in all things God works for the good of those who love him, who have been called according to his purpose.'I trust you God. He is so small, so…" I whispered, the words catching in my throat. "Keep him with us. Just let him hold on a little longer." I stayed there, a silent sentinel in the dark, waiting for a miracle,a knock on the door.

I rushed to open the door and welcomed Dr. Fraser in and quickly led him upstairs to Angus's room. As I pulled back the blankets and revealed Angus's small, feverish form, I saw the worry deepen on the doctor's face. His brow furrowed in confusion and concern. Without wasting any time, Dr. Fraser reached into his bag, pulled out a thermometer, and gently pressed it underneath Angus's tongue. I watched closely, hoping for good news. A few seconds later, the doctor carefully removed the thermometer and looked at the mercury. His eyes widened with concern. It was clear from his expression that this was serious. The room grew even quieter, filled only with the muffled sounds of Angus's restless breathing and the disheartening sighs of the doctor. I knew then that we needed to act fast.

Dr. Fraser examined the boy carefully, noting that his fever wasn't dangerously high, but it was elevated enough to require quick action. The doctor's steady hands pressed lightly on Angus's forehead, checking for sweat, while his brows furrowed in concern. He explained that the body could sometimes fight off infection better if it was not overwhelmed with heat, so cooling measures were essential.

Before leaving, Dr. Fraser handed me a small glass container filled with a light, fragrant liquid made from meadowsweet, a plant known for its calming and fever-reducing qualities. The aroma of the potion hinted at natural healing, and I watched him with quiet respect. He gave me clear instructions: give Angus two small spoonfuls of the meadowsweet brew every three hours. His voice was calm but firm, emphasizing the importance of sticking to this schedule without fail. I nodded, feeling the weight of responsibility settle on my shoulders. The doctor then explained that this remedy, combined with efforts to keep him cool—like sponging his forehead and keeping him in a shaded, breezy room—would help bring his fever down more steadily.

Days passed slowly. For four days, I monitored Angus closely, following every instruction without missing a single dose. During those long hours, I watched his small chest rise and fall, praying the fever wouldn't spike again. I noted every change: a slight shift in his coloring, a faint flicker of movement here and there. And then, on that fourth day, I noticed something different. His fever finally broke. The body that had been so tense and hot now began to relax. His brow softened, and he slowly started to regain consciousness. A faint sparkle appeared in his eyes, and I felt a wave of relief wash over me.

Still, that night haunted me. I remembered how delirious he had been during those fevered dreams. His mind had wandered into strange nightmares, filled with shadows and whispers I couldn't reach. Those moments of helplessness pressed heavily in my chest. I took a deep breath, fighting back tears, and settled into the chair beside his bed.

Several days passed before I was finally able to return to work, Angus still by my side. It struck me how quickly he had managed to find a place in the hardened hearts of the Scotland Yard detectives and Constables. I hadn't realized just how deeply he had touched them until I started receiving multiple phone calls from headquarters. The calls came in one after another, questions filled with concern about Angus' well-being. These Constables, who usually appeared tough and unreadable, showed clear signs of care. They understood that, no matter how small, Angus was at the heart of the case, that his well-being could lead us closer to the truth. Each call served as a reminder that, while we were all focused on solving a difficult puzzle. Their efforts to find connections in Angus' mother's murder and the mystery surrounding his father were relentless, and their compassion gave me hope that we would uncover the truth soon.

The same calls also reassured me that the team was fully committed to the case. They had informed me that someone had come forward and was willing to share information with us, but that the informant would not give their name. The constable's words felt like a promise—they were determined to find out what really happened.

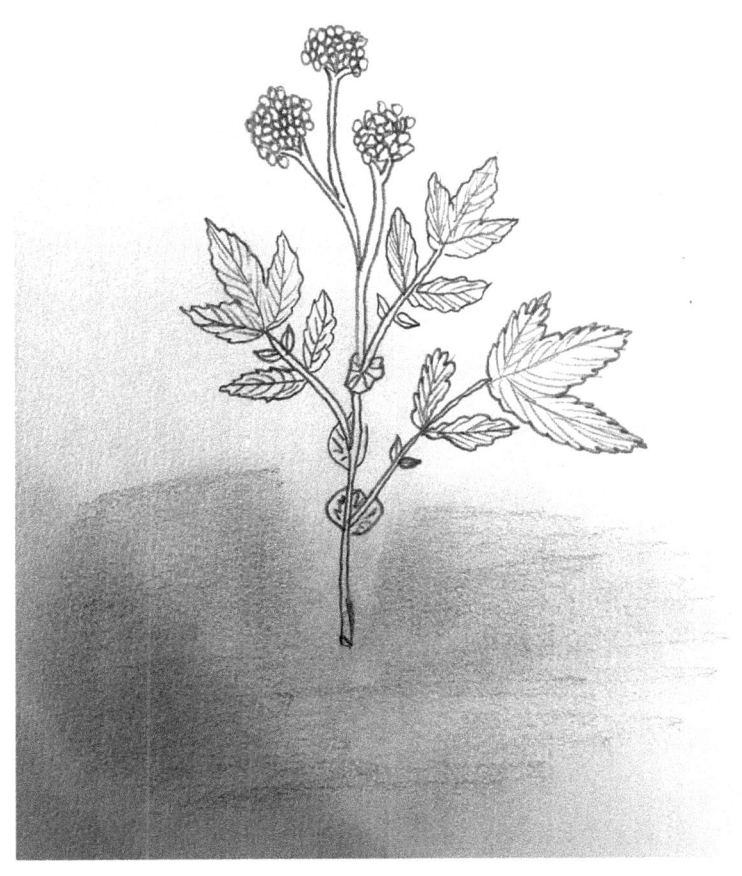

CASE FILE# 000010

CASE MANAGER: BRIANNA BAIRD

LEAD AGENT: GORDON McCurr

SUBJECT: Angus O'Connor

After I dropped Angus off at the station
with Detective Rachel Bishop, I took a
moment to reassure him. I told him I'd be
back soon and didn't need to worry. Then, I
set out on my own journey to find the
mysterious informant's address. The walk was
short but tense, lined with empty streets
that seemed to hold their own secrets. When
I finally arrived at the appointed address,
I was rather surprised to find that I was
outside of the Edinburgh Library, after
taking a cursory glance at my surroundings,
I spotted her— a woman stood her hands
trembling slightly as her eyes darted around
the people passing by. Her head turning from
side to side as she analyzed everyone one
close to her as if worried someone was
watching. She looked like someone who was

expecting something to happen, though I wasn't sure what.

I approached her carefully, not wanting to startle her. I gently asked if she was the woman who had called me earlier. She hesitated for a second before giving me a small nod of her head. Her eyes widened just a little, revealing how uneasy she truly was. I then asked if she had seen who left the O'Connor family's house that night. Her face flickered with worry as she responded. She told me she saw a man running out of their home, but her words came slowly, as if she was trying to recall that night in finer detail. She admitted it was dark and difficult to see, which made her uncertain about identifying who he was. She said she couldn't be sure if she recognised him or if she could pick him out of a group of people, just that he was a man and had a limp. My stomach tightened when her words sank in. She had seen someone, a figure fleeing the house, but she couldn't give a solid description. Her statement felt like a punch to the chest, a hint of a crucial piece of the puzzle slipping away. My jaw clenched in frustration, I had hoped that this witness might have been able to give me something more concrete— a man with a limp was hardly a rare description.

Something about her hesitation lingered in my mind, and I couldn't help but wonder how much she truly remembered or had been able to see in that dark, cold night, leaving me with more questions than answers.

I studied her closely, trying to read the small signs that she might be hiding something. Her eyes darted around nervously, moving quickly from one spot to another, as if she was afraid someone might catch her in a lie. Her hands trembled slightly, and she kept fidgeting with her sleeve, an unconscious sign of her anxiety. I knew she wasn't comfortable, and it was clear she was holding things back. It was as if she carried a heavy secret she wasn't ready to give up, no matter how much I pressed her. Her fear was obvious, and I could see it in her wary glances, her quick breaths, and the tight way she bit her lip.

Realizing I needed to find a way to get her to open up, I decided to approach her differently. I asked calmly if she wanted to come down to the station with me. I explained that I only wanted to get a formal statement—a simple record of what she knew. I told her it might help clarify things and possibly reveal important clues. Her face flickered at the mention of the station. One second she looked like she was thinking things over, and the next, her eyes suddenly filled with fear. It was as if I'd touched on something she was desperate to hide. Instead of answering immediately, she looked past me, out into the darkness beyond us. Her entire posture changed. It was like she was seeing something invisible, something only she could see. Her eyes widened slightly, and her breathing grew faster. The

fear on her face deepened, and I could feel
that whatever she saw or thought about
terrified her even more than before.

Curious, I turned around slowly to see
what had captured her attention. I didn't
rush. I wanted to see what made her freeze
up. When I looked behind me, I noticed a
faint glint in the shadows—a tiny sparkle
that caught the low light in a deviant way.
It was small, but powerful enough to stand
out. It reminded me of a shiny knife or a
small blade, hidden just out of sight. That
little flicker told me everything I needed
to understand. She was too frightened to
speak freely. Her silence wasn't just about
being nervous or stubborn; it was about
being terrified of what might happen if she
talked. She was worried about revealing the
truth or exposing herself, or perhaps she
was afraid someone was watching her closely.
The sparkle in the shadows made it clear
that danger was lurking.

After a few moments of strained silence, I softened my tone. I lowered my voice and tried to sound reassuring. I told her quietly that she could stop by my house later. I said we could talk there, away from eyes and ears that might be listening. Watching her, I saw her rigid shoulders relax just a bit. She nodded slightly, though her face still looked taut with worry. She wasn't fully convinced, but she was willing to trust me enough to give it a try.

Carefully, I turned back and began walking toward the station. I contemplated the various ways I knew to instil trust in a witness in order to gain the full story. Her silence spoke loudly. I knew she was holding back secrets she didn't want anyone to uncover, but undoubtedly those secrets needed to come to light. I could tell she was weighing the risks of talking against staying quiet. Whatever the details, I knew these secrets held weight. They were not

small, and they had the power to shift
everything we thought we knew.

As my mind reeling with all the
information that I was given. I heard a
small tap-tap-tap as if someone were walking
with a cane behind me. I turned around and
all I saw was the empty street behind me.
Feeling the hairs on the back of my neck
raise, I continued on my journey, feeling
slightly on edge when the tapping returned
with a faster pace. I turned back again and
saw the shadow of a figure duck into the
passageway. My heart leapt through my chest,
my step quickened. I found myself memorizing
each face around me and looking for anyone
who may be following me further.

CASE FILE# 000011

CASE MANAGER: BRIANNA BAIRD

LEAD AGENT: GORDON McCurr

SUBJECT: Angus O'Connor

Many long hours had gone by since
Angus and I first arrived at
headquarters. The building was swarming
with activity. I had finally finished
my reports and completed all the
necessary formalities. Exhausted my
legs felt like they could give way at
any moment. I was eager to get out of
there and head home, to find some peace
after the chaos of the day and so was
Angus.

Stepping outside, the cool air hit us. It
was a breath of fresh air, calming and still
compared to the madness behind us. The
city's hum was quieter now, the rush of
people less intense. It felt like stepping
into a different world. The street was dark,
lit only by flickering streetlamps casting

long shadows. We started walking along the dimly lit street, each footstep echoing softly on the cracked cobbles. Just then, the peace was shattered by a voice so loud it seemed to tear through the calm.

A constable, waving his arms wildly, yelled out urgently. His face was distorted, eyes wide with fear, and his voice echoed loudly through the quiet night. He called for help, shouting about a robbery suspect fleeing through the alleyways nearby. His words were clear but frantic, alerting anyone within ear shot to the danger. As he yelled, his arms swung wildly, trying to point us toward the chaos. His voice carried over the faint sounds of the city, making my heart race. The urgency in his cry made it clear that this was a situation I couldn't ignore. Without thinking, my instincts kicked in. I spun around, recognizing the danger immediately. I looked at Angus, my voice firm, telling him to run back toward

the station. I urged him to stay safe and
alert the Constables waiting there.

But even as I spoke, I saw something in
his face that made me hesitate. Instead of
turning to run, Angus stood frozen in place.
His body shuddered uncontrollably. His wide
eyes reflected pure fear, and his lips
trembled as if he wanted to scream but
couldn't. The sudden sound of gunfire
shattered the fragile calm. It echoed
through the narrow alley like a nightmare.
The sky seemed to explode with flashes of
light as bullets rained down. The shots
ricocheted off the lined walls and
deafeningly struck the wooden barrels that
lined the alley's edges. People would have
thought the very world was falling apart.

Fear gripped my chest hard enough to make
breathing difficult. My mind turned blank
but focused all at once. A bullet whistled
past me, singing through the air like a
deadly note, hitting a wooden barrel nearby.
Another sharp bang of a gunshot flooded my

veins with adrenaline. Without hesitation, I snapped into action. I threw my arms beneath Angus's trembling body, lifting him carefully off the ground. His small frame was shivering so much that I worried he might slip from my grasp. His forehead was slick with sweat, and his eyes looked haunted, blank with terror. The look in his eyes told me more than I'd seen before.

Quickly, I pulled him behind a stack of shipping crates, trying to hide him from the chaos. I pressed him flat against the cold, hard metal and worn wood, hoping the makeshift barrier would shield him from stray bullets. I turned sharply on my heel and pushed forward. Ignoring my own fear, I ran after the armed robber, dodging behind the piles of broken boxes and scattered debris. The suspect was hunched low, darting through the alley to avoid the gunfire. You could see the panic in his movements as he ducked behind crates, barrels, and anything else he could hide behind.

It was all pure instinct. I knew I couldn't stop. I had to keep moving, no matter how loud the bullets screamed past or how heavy the chaos felt. The bullets kept firing, bouncing off metal and whizzing through the air like deadly firecrackers. The alley was a tight maze, with deafening echoes and sharp corners that could easily swallow me whole. I kept low to the ground, following his zigzagging path. He darted left then right, trying to dodge the gunfire that seemed to come from everywhere at once. The noise was disorentating—the crack of gunfire, the ricochets echoing, and debris flying through the air like deadly shrapnel. Every second felt like I was fighting to stay focused amid the frenzy. My senses were stretched thin, and it was a struggle to remember to breathe.

The narrow space of the alley made it easy to get lost or ambushed. I kept my eyes fixed on the suspect, watching every move he made. I moved quietly, fluidly, trying not to be seen. Every step I took felt like a risk, but stopping wasn't an option. The criminal serpantined, trying to break the line between us and put more distance between himself and the danger. I pushed on, forcing myself past the scattered debris and broken glass. I knew I had to catch him before another shot was fired—or worse, before someone else got hurt.

This was life or death. Every movement, every breath, every decision mattered. I stayed low, kept my eyes sharp, and kept chasing. The criminal moved fast, slipping through a shadowed crawlspace, ducking behind a pile of broken whiskey barrels. I followed, slipping through the debris. Breathing hard from the exertion, I quickly veered left to cut him off and paused, watching him approach. I held my breath, waiting for just the right moment. He was almost close enough to see. As soon as I saw him pass by, I made my move. I darted from my hiding spot, lunging behind him and

colliding with his back. With a firm grip, I
pinned him to the wet, uneven street, the
dampness making the cobbles slick as I
tightened my hold on him. My hands moved
quickly, cuffing him with cold, metal
restraints. Without hesitation, I grabbed
his arm and tugged him upright, forcing him
to face me. I then guided him to the nearby
constable standing at the street corner. My
voice was steady but firm as I explained
that I needed to leave quickly to fetch
Angus. I assured the constable that I would
return to fill out the official reports at
the station after I located the boy. I was
only a short distance away from where I had
left Angus. I dropped to my knees beside
him, trying hard to bring him back to the
present moment. His breathing was fast and
uneven.

Carefully, I reached out and gently wiped
away the tears still falling down his face.
He reached out and grabbed me in a

desperate, tight embrace, as if holding on for dear life.

"Angus," I whispered, my voice a gravelly rumble, trying to cut through the fog of his fear.

"It's over, lad. It's over," I murmured, gently but firmly pulling him into my chest, cradling his shaking head. He buried his face in my coat, his sobs muffled but violent. "Just breathe, son. Breathe with me." I felt the frantic beat of his heart against my ribs.

"I… I thought…" he choked out, the words catching in his throat.

"I know what you thought," I said, stroking his hair, feeling the dampness of his tears through the rough fabric. "It was a close call, a devillish dance. But you're safe now. I'm here." I closed my eyes for a moment.

"Peace I leave with you; my peace I give you. I do not give to you as the world gives. Do not let your hearts be troubled

and do not be afraid. Those are the words
the Lord gave us in John 14:27. Hold fast to
those words lad, they will see us through."

He stirred, his breathing slowly evening
out, the tremors subsiding. He looked up,
his eyes still red-rimmed but a flicker of
understanding dawning. "Peace, Angus," I
repeated, holding him tighter. "We'll find
it. Together." We had only traveled about
halfway to Scotland Yard when shifted my
hold on Angus and noticed Angus's head
begin to droop against my shoulder, his
eyelids growing heavier with each step.
Before I knew it, he had slipped into an
exhausted, uneasy sleep. His tiny chest rose
and fell unevenly. Once we reached Scotland
Yard headquarters, I carefully set Angus
down on the chair at my desk where he curled
into the back of it as tightly as he could,
seeking comfort in the faint warmth of the
office.

I then made my way down the hall to the
lead detective's office. My steps were

steady but filled with a sense of urgency. Inside, I explained in detail what had happened during the chase and capture of the suspect we'd spent the last two months tracking. I described how we had positioned ourselves, how the suspect, Tobias Matthews, had fought to escape at the last moment. I told him about the moment when we finally cornered him, the quick decision to arrest him, and the dangerous situation we faced. I emphasized how elusive Matthews had been, disappearing into the shadows at crucial times and slipping past our best efforts to catch him.

Tobias Matthews was no ordinary criminal. His record shows he's previously been arrested for armed robbery, where he held up a small jewelry store in the city with a loaded gun. He also committed arson, setting fire to a warehouse in an attempt to cover his tracks during an earlier theft. On top of that, Matthews was charged as an accessory to kidnapping, linking him to a crime where a man was taken against his will. His history is filled with violent and reckless crimes that made him dangerous and hard to pin down. Knowing who he was made the recent capture even more significant. We'd been on his trail long enough to see his tricks—his quick getaway tactics, his tendency to switch disguises, and how he always seemed to be one step ahead. Our team had needed to be sharp, patient, and persistent. Now, with him caught, we could finally start to piece together the full picture of his past crimes and move closer to bringing him to justice. The stress in the room was thick, but I knew this was just another step in a long fight to keep the streets safe.

After I had gone through several sheets of paperwork and carefully examined my notes on the Iris O'Connor murder case, I felt a strong need to bring Angus home. It was late in the day, and my mind was full of details and questions that still needed answers. The long hours of reading and cross-referencing had left me mentally exhausted. I walked slowly over to my desk, the papers scattered across it like a messy puzzle waiting to be solved. Gently, I nudged Angus with my hand, trying to rouse him. His eyes fluttered open slowly, and for a moment, he looked disoriented, as if the weight of the day's events was pressing down on him. I gave him a soft word of reassurance, knowing he was more stressed than he let on.

When we finally arrived home, I headed straight to the kitchen to prepare a meal that was not just quick, but slightly healthier than my usual fare. I kept it simple—steamed vegetables, a small portion of lean chicken, and some fresh bread. I watched as Angus ate with quiet appreciation, knowing he'd soon be back on his feet. After he finished his dinner, I guided him gently toward the staircase. I made sure the room was warm and dimly lit, just enough to help him relax. I spoke softly, encouraging him to settle in for the night, and placed a blanket over him. Watching him settle into bed made me feel a bit better about the pandemonium of the day. It was clear to me that rest was necessary if we were to handle the challenges ahead.

With a deep breath, I turned out the lights and made my way back downstairs. The house was quiet now, except for the faint sounds of Angus breathing softly in the next room. I sat down for a moment, thinking about the case and everything that still needed to be done. But for now, I knew he was safe. That was enough.

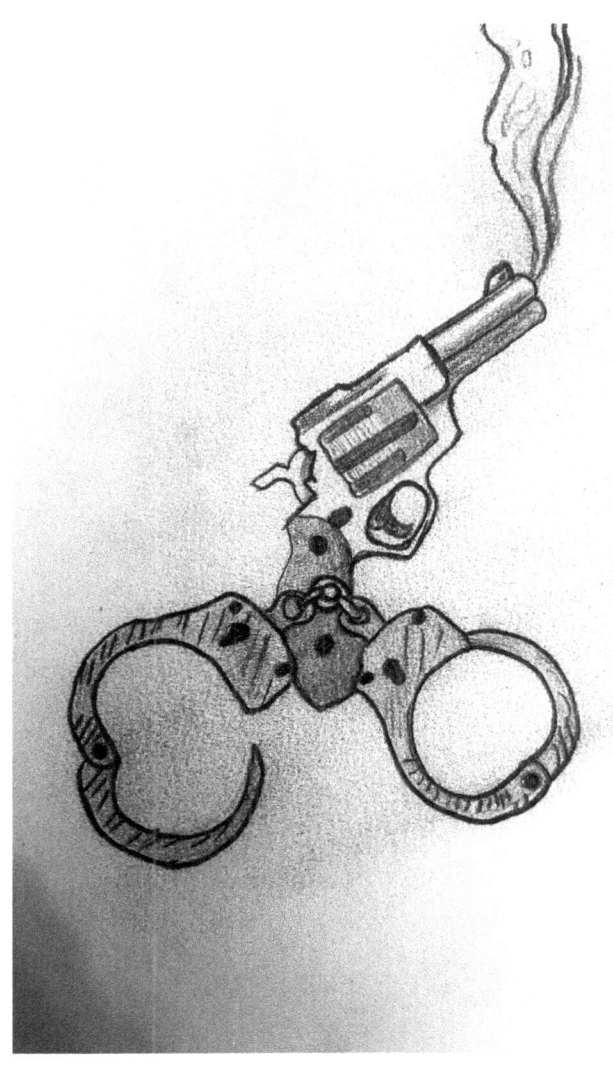

CASE FILE# 000012

CASE MANAGER: BRIANNA BAIRD

LEAD AGENT: GORDON McCurr

SUBJECT: Angus O'Connor

    The night was eerily quiet, almost too quiet. No wind rustled through the trees. No distant hooves or sounds of the night echoed through the streets. It was as if the world had paused in stillness. Inside, a thick hush settled over the house, making every creak or faint noise seem unnaturally loud. I stood there, feeling a strange mix of calm and dread, knowing something was wrong. But what I didn't expect was to find Angus missing. His absence hit harder than I thought it would. My mind raced, trying to make sense of it all. I started by checking his bed first. The sheets were smooth, perfectly made—no sign of him moving around or trying to hide. The room was silent, the quiet feeling even more intense. No toys, no clothes, no clues left behind. I moved quickly but carefully, my heart pounding painfully in my chest. Then I checked downstairs. I looked in every room—the kitchen, the living room, even outside in the backyard. Nothing. No sign of Angus anywhere around the house. It was as if he had vanished into thin air, evaporated without a trace. My stomach clenched tightly, but I fought to stay calm, to keep my mind clear. I knew I had to act quickly. My instincts told me that every second counted.

Moving with purpose, I headed towards the O'Connor house, fearing that Angus had gone back there. Maybe, in his confusion or panic, he returned to the only place that felt familiar—his mother's old crime scene, a place that had haunted him ever since her murder just a month ago. As I drew closer, a strange, sinking feeling grew in my gut. The deeper I went, the more I felt that something was terribly wrong. I told myself to stay focused, but the nagging panic was hard to push aside. I searched room by room, opening closets, peeking behind furniture, calling his name—but each space only echoed with the same oppressive silence. No toys, no clothes, no clues. Just emptiness. The clock was relentless, reminding me time was slipping away. I knew I had to find him before it was too late. Reaching the end of the hallway, I grabbed the phone. My fingers trembled slightly as I lifted the receiver and waited for the operator. When the operator asked for direction I gave direction to a number near London close to White Chapel, it was to Detective Abberline the Detective and leader of our secret sector of Scotland Yard. I waited for him to answer as one ring passed and then another. He sounded haggard when he picked up the line, without waiting for him to ask, I explained quickly that Angus was missing. I knew he would assign the resources I would need to canvas the neighborhood and surrounding area if he were made aware of the urgency behind the call. Abberline, as predicted, was quick to agree and I heard him murmur something about "The Ripper" before the call ended on his side. Knowing I had assistance coming, I forced myself to leave the O'Connor house.

My legs moved on their own accord, each step faster than the last. I waited outside for the other detectives to arrive, knowing they'd bring better tools, sharper eyes, and more experience. When they finally got there, we moved through the house together.

Methodically, we checked every room, every corner. Then we reached Angus's room, and my breath caught in my throat. I couldn't believe what I saw. Sitting on his desk, in the corner of the room, was a small rag. It appeared plain, nothing special about it, but there was something unsettling about it. I noticed a faint smudge on the fabric. A sickly sweet smell wafted from it, oddly calming yet disturbing. At first, it

was faint, almost like a whisper, but I
recognized the scent immediately. I'd read
about it, but I had never encountered it
myself—chloroform. The word hung heavy in my
mind. The realization hit me like a punch.
That chemical, the same one used to knock
someone unconscious, was right there, right
in the boy's room. A cold wave of fear
washed over me. My skin prickled with dread.
My stomach twisted as the sinister truth
sank in. Something darker was at play here.
This wasn't just about a lost boy. It was
about something much worse. I could feel it
pressing against the back of my mind,
waiting to be uncovered. The night seemed to
stretch endlessly before me, filled with
questions I couldn't answer yet. Every
detail told a story that wasn't finished.
The quiet, the scent, the missing boy—all
signs of a situation far more dangerous and
sinister than I had imagined. I pleaded
silently, *Lord help me find him before it
is too late..*

The inspectors studied the rag with
great care. Their eyes moved over every
frayed edge and stain on the fabric. One of
them, faster than the rest, hurried to the
corridor phone. He grabbed it quickly,
almost clutching it in his hand. Without
wasting a second, he picked up the receiver
and called the switchboard for the chief
inspector. The call was brief but serious;
he began to report what looked like an
official kidnapping.

It wasn't long before I finally got
into the chief inspector's office. The
moment I stepped inside, the atmosphere
shifted. The room felt electric, charged
with importance and pressure. Footsteps
echoed loudly outside as other Constables
moved by quickly. Their muffled voices
barely reached us, but the sense of urgency
was clear. The chief inspector was pacing
back and forth across his small office. His
face was lined, the lines telling stories of
long hours and worries. His brow was deeply

furrowed. Every so often, he paused rubbing his jaw as if lost in thought. His eyes betrayed how deeply he cared. They darted nervously to the door whenever he paused, as if he expected news at any second. His expression was serious, but beneath that, I saw worry. Deep down, I could tell he was afraid for Angus.

When I finally pushed open the door and stepped inside, the chief inspector stopped pacing instantly. His gaze locked onto mine. His eyes, tired but sharp, revealing— He took a deep breath, steadying himself. Without hesitation, he looked straight into my eyes and spoke with firm authority. "All of your other duties are to be put on hold until Angus is back safe and sound, where he belongs." His words weren't just words. They were a command driven by true concern. He made it clear that the boy's safety was now the hightest priority. Everyone in the room understood the urgency and seriousness. Angus's safety was no longer a matter of routine. It was a matter of the heart. And at that moment, everyone in the building was united by one simple, clear goal: find Angus and bring him home safe.

A wave of relief washed over me as those words finally reached my ears. It was as if a heavy weight had suddenly been lifted from my chest, leaving me with a clear mind and a renewed sense of purpose. I knew in my gut that he had been taken by force. The clues in that moment confirmed my fear.

The open window told its own dark story. It had been locked before I went to bed, so how could it be open now? The marks on the sash and the bent lock mechanism were unmistakable signs of a forced entry. Someone, someone who knew this was *his* room, had broken in deliberately. The window had been tampered with, jimmied open with tools that someone brought along. The evidence suggested they had used

something like a ships bar or a flat
tool to pry it open. Once the window
was compromised, the perpetrator was
able to crawl inside with ease.

I imagined it. A figure lurking in
the dark, watching for the right moment
to take the boy quietly, almost
silently. The intruder would have
entered swiftly, knowing exactly what
they needed. They had likely planned
it, bringing the right tools to break
in without making too much noise. The
goal would have been to grab him and
carry him out before anyone noticed.
Given how easily the window opened, it
would have been simple for them to
crawl through with the boy unconscious
or too scared to fight back. I pictured
the scene in my mind—the boy limp and
quiet, the kidnapper carefully lifting
him to avoid waking him, then slipping
out into the night. No matter how much

I prayed I was wrong, I knew that this
was not a random act.

I couldn't remove the feeling that
the note I was sent almost a month ago
led to this moment; they knew exactly
where to find him, and I was at fault.
They avoided drawing attention until it
was too late. Now, the question was how
he was—was he hurt? Was he scared? Was
he crying somewhere, alone? *God keep
him safe, protect him from harm, help
me find him quickly*. My mind kept
racing over these questions as I clung
to the only certainty I had—that
someone had broken in with intent, and
now I had to find him before anything
worse happened.

CASE FILE# 000013

CASE MANAGER: BRIANNA BAIRD

LEAD AGENT: GORDON McCurr

SUBJECT: Angus O'Connor

It had already been two long days since I first started hunting for little Angus, and the hope that I might find him alive was beginning to fade. Every moment felt heavier with doubt. I had exhausted almost all my leads, the clues I chased leaving me with just one last possibility. Still, I couldn't shake the gnawing worry about Angus's safety. He had been taken against his will, forced away from everything familiar. Now, he was with someone he didn't trust, probably scared, unsure of what awaited him. The thought of him trapped with a stranger, made my chest constrict. I knew he didn't belong there. The fear of what might be happening to him haunted me each day and night.

With heavy steps, I made my way down the quiet street toward the abandoned warehouse that we'd been watching for the past two days. It was an old building, with broken windows and a door that hung slightly off its hinges. I had been paying close attention to the comings and goings, noting only one familiar figure entering early in the morning and leaving late at night. That person's routine seemed suspicious, almost robotic, which only deepened my concern. Every detail mattered—each movement, each glance. When I finally reached the entrance, I hesitated for just a moment, then pushed the door open, each creak sounding unnaturally loud in the silence. I stepped inside with cautious confidence, listening intently once the door was closed behind me. I needed to catch any sound inside—voices, footsteps, even the faintest cry.

As I moved deeper into the dark, empty space, my senses sharpened. Suddenly, I heard a small whimper—a sound pure with fear—and then a disturbing, stirring laugh that could only be described as insane. My heart began pounding harder, adrenaline flooding my veins. Instead of feeling fear, something fiery ignited inside me— a righteous anger at whoever had hurt Angus and frustration at how helpless I felt. I quickened my pace around a corner, desperate to find him. That's when I saw it—the terror in his eyes as tears streamed down his face. Angus was tightly bound to a cold, metal chair, his tiny body trembling. I took a few seconds to really look at the situation. The room was dim; shadows gathered along its rough, stone walls. The flickering lamp overhead cast a faint glow, revealing the ropes that held him firmly in place. His small hands tugged at the bindings, nails digging into the rough fabric. His wide eyes darted around, searching for something familiar—anything to give him strength. The rag stuffed inside his mouth looked dirty, smudged with grime, and the edges were torn from repeated use. The corners of his lips twitched in panic, and tears continued to fall freely. My gut twisted with a mix of fury and indignation. I knew I had to act fast before something worse happened. Right then, my mind cleared enough to understand that this moment could turn dark very quickly. Every second counted. My focus sharpened as I prepared to find a way to free him and get him out of danger. *Lord help keep him safe.*

Suddenly, the man who had been coming in and out of the building for the past two days turned a corner with clear purpose. He moved swiftly, as if he knew exactly where he was headed. He didn't even glance in my direction his focus seemed fixed on something only he understood. As he reached the middle of the warehouse, and suddenly halted. Without hesitation, he spun on his heels and faced me, eyes wild and crazed. A maniacal gleam flickered in his stare, reflecting his unstable state. His expression was intense, almost frightening, as if he had lost all control.

He stared at me for a long second before something shifted. The madness in his eyes ignited, fueling his anger. Without warning, he shot forward with explosive speed, fists clenched tightly. His arm swung towards my face in a violent burst, clearly driven by rage. I saw his fist tighten and then felt it crash into my jaw with brutal force. A sharp pain erupted in my skull, spreading quickly through my veins. It startled me so much that I lost my balance and fell hard onto the cold, hard floor. The impact made my head ring and my body ache. My ears buzzed, and for a moment, I struggled just to stay conscious.

From where I lay, I could see the man standing before me. He was still breathing hard, his chest heaving with each ragged breath. His face was tense with fury, but I could see something else—something wild and unhinged in his expression. His breath was visible in the icy air, swirling around him like a ghostly fog. It was sharp and cold enough to freeze the space between us, creating a thick, fog-like barrier that seemed to separate him from any sense or reason. The freezing air clung to the scene, making it feel even more tense and unforgiving.

Taking a fleeting chance, I pushed myself up, ignoring the throbbing pain in my jaw and head. My instincts kicked in. I saw my moment, it was a miracle given from God, and I seized it. With quick, determined steps, I rushed toward Angus, who was still trapped and helpless. I reached him just in time and without hesitation, I worked quickly to untie the ropes binding him. My hands trembled but stayed steady as I worked quickly to free him. Once loose, I carefully lifted the boy into my arms—the limp weight of him telling me he was losing strength fast.

I didn't hesitate. I turned and ran as fast as I could, clutching Angus close. My heart pounded in my chest. With one final burst of energy, I carried the boy out of the warehouse, leaving behind the chaos and danger. My mind was clear and focused on one thing—getting Argus to safety before it was too late.

CASE FILE# 000014

CASE MANAGER: BRIANNA BAIRD

LEAD AGENT: GORDON McCurr

SUBJECT: Angus O'Connor

When I reached the heavy, creaking door, I hesitated for a moment. I glanced back over my shoulder, expecting to see the man still there, still watching. To my surprise, he had vanished completely, as if swallowed by the shadows. A shiver ran down my spine. An uneasy feeling settled in my chest. I wondered how he managed to slip away unseen so quickly. Had he really been there at all, or was he just a hallucination? My thoughts raced as I fought to stay focused. I shook off the worry, but it lingered deep inside, gnawing at me.

My attention quickly shifted to Angus. He was unconscious now, lying there on the cold ground. I hurried to bend down and carefully lift him, being mindful not to

hurt him further. His small frame was
surprisingly fragile, and I could see how
exhausted and scared he looked even asleep.
I carefully cradled him in my arms and
rushed toward the hospital, my mind working
furiously. The warehouse, where all this
chaos had happened, was only a short walk
away, no more than a few hundred paces. It
only took seconds of brisk walking to reach
the hospital entrance.

As I entered, tension built inside me.
I guided Angus directly into an exam room,
and I held my breath. I watched anxiously as
the doctor moved quickly to examine him.
Every detail felt amplified—each second
seemed longer than the one before. I
couldn't help but think about how fragile he
looked, barely able to stay alive after just
a short period of unconsciousness. My heart
pounded with hope and fear at the same time.
I kept my eyes on the doctor, waiting for
some sign of what was wrong. When the doctor
finally looked up and turned to me, a soft

sigh escaped my lips. Relief flooded through me when he said Angus had only fainted because of the stress—a temporary reaction, no lasting damage.

It was hours before I was able to bring Angus home. During that time, I stayed close, watching over him like a hawk. I kept thinking about how easily things could have gone wrong that day. His fainting spell had been sudden and frightening. But now, I knew he was safe, at least for the moment. The long hours in the hospital had been tiring, but seeing him resting peacefully in my home would make it all worth it. I felt grateful that he was going to be okay. God had answered my prayers.

When we finally pulled up outside my house, I could see how exhausted Angus looked. His small body moved slowly, almost as if he was barely able to lift his legs. His face was tired, with lines of fatigue etched deep from the long, tense day. Without waiting, I directed him to his room,

telling him softly but firmly to go get
ready for bed. He moved slowly, and once
inside, I watched as he disappeared behind
the door, already looking like sleep was
pulling him under.

As soon as he was gone, I rang
headquarters. I needed to make sure every
detail of what had happened at the warehouse
was fully understood. I explained carefully,
piece by piece, what Angus had seen and what
he remembered. I described his movements,
the expressions on his face, and how he had
felt during those tense moments. I wanted
them to get a complete picture so they could
understand exactly what had taken place. I
underlined the crucial parts, emphasizing
where he saw the figure, how his heart
pounded, and how frozen he had been with
fear. Every word I said mattered because
this information could be what led to
finding the man responsible.

Once I finished the call, I climbed the
stairs slowly, my mind heavy with everything

I'd just shared. When I reached Angus's door again, I gently knocked before opening it just a crack. Inside, I saw him sitting up in bed, eyes half-closed, eyelids heavy. I leaned in close and softly told him he needed to speak with the head detective at headquarters. I explained how important it was for him to share everything he could remember, any details that might lend themselves to the investigation and capture of his kidnapper. I told Angus that sharing his memories could make a difference, that it could help keep him safe and possibly prevent this from happening again. His eyes fluttered open slightly, and he nodded faintly, as if he was already drifting toward sleep.

I reached over his bed and gently pulled the covers up around him, tucking them softly beneath his chin. I couldn't help but softly ruffle his messy hair, a small act of comfort in a night filled with unknowns. Carefully, I eased out of the room, tiptoeing across the hall so I wouldn't wake him fully. I left his door slightly open, just enough so if he needed me, I would hear him.

I was about to close my eyes and try to rest when suddenly, the quiet night shattered with loud, desperate shouts. The noise snapped through the stillness, and in an instant, my heart pounded fiercely in my chest. A blast of fear shot through me, making every nerve stand on end. Without thinking, I leapt out of bed and hurried across the hall into Angus's room. There, I saw him sitting up, his small body trembled uncontrollably—not from the cold, but from pure terror. I thought about the man who had hurt Angus mentally, the one who had caused so much fear, and realized he was still out there. Somehow, he had slipped away again. The anger and regret tore through me like a storm.

The next morning, I woke before dawn,
the house still wrapped in quiet darkness. I
moved softly, as if afraid to wake the
world. I quietly stepped into Angus's room,
relieved to find him sleeping soundly. With
care, I gently shook his shoulder,
whispering his name softly to rouse him. His
eyelids fluttered open, and he blinked
groggily at the light, stretching his limbs
slowly before sitting up. After getting him
settled, I made my way downstairs. The house
was still quiet, the air filled with the
aroma of fresh cooking. I started to prepare
breakfast, knowing a warm meal would lift
our spirits. I got out flour, baking soda,
and raisins to make tattie scones — a
simple, hearty treat. The sound of Lorne
sausage sizzling on the stove. I poured a
glass of fresh milk for Angus, knowing how
much he liked it. As I finished preparing
breakfast, I looked up to see Angus making
his slow way down the stairs, rubbing his
eyes and yawning. His face showed a mix of

169

tiredness and gratitude. I knew the day
ahead might still hold challenges, but for
now, we had this quiet moment of peace,
built on careful hope and the simple comfort
of a good breakfast shared between us.

As we sat down to enjoy our meal, I
found my mind drifting to Angus. I
realized that whenever I had to leave
the headquarters for a while, he
couldn't stay behind. I started to
think about possible options for him
during the day when I was away. Could
he go somewhere safe? Would he be
happy? I looked around the small room,
feeling unsure. My eyes drifted toward
the windows, which were covered by
plain curtains. Through the thin gaps,
I caught sight of a line of children
walking down the street, some with
satchels, others holding hands with
parents. They looked so small and
eager, some smiling, others deep in
thought, as they made their way to

school. Watching them, a sudden thought struck me as clear as sunlight. Angus needed to learn, to go to school like other children his age. It dawned on me that giving him an education could solve more than one problem at once. If I sent him to school, he would be safe, occupied, and learning every day. That would keep him out of trouble and give him something meaningful to do. I looked at Angus more closely now, noticing his puzzled expression. His brow was furrowed, and his eyes flicked from the window to me, as if trying to understand what had grabbed my attention. A small smile crept onto my lips when I saw his confusion. It was comforting, even a little amusing, to see him trying to make sense of what was happening around him. The idea of sending him to school felt like the right step. It was a simple solution that could fix a lot of issues at once.

I quickly explained to Angus that he would need to start school soon since the new semester had already begun. I could see the fear creeping into his eyes as I talked. He looked overwhelmed, as if the idea of being in a new place with unfamiliar faces was enough to terrify him. I tried to reassure him, but my words felt small against the storm of worry he was already feeling. His mind was clearly racing with questions, every doubt flashing across his face. I could see him imagining all sorts of terrible scenarios—what if he got lost, or someone hurt him, or something worse? He looked at me with wide eyes that shimmered with uncertaintly, and in a quiet voice, he asked what would happen if the man came back. His voice was barely above a whisper, trembling as he brought up the possibility I had hoped wouldn't cross his mind.

That simple question hit me hard. I
hadn't prepared myself for that worry
to surface now, not so soon. What if
that man did come back, and what if he
decided to try and snatch Angus from
the school? Could I really protect him?
Would the teachers be able to keep him
safe? These questions swirled in my
head. I remembered how a single moment
of distraction or a lapse in security
could turn dangerous.

The image of that man returning was
enough to make my mind race with
worst-case scenarios. I thought about
how crowded the school was—kids running
around, parents dropping off their
children, teachers focused on their
lessons—yet I couldn't shake the fear
that the man could slip through all
those cracks. I wondered what plans, if
any, were in place to keep children
like Angus safe from someone who might
want to hurt them. Anxiety grew

stronger as I pictured him being taken away before I could do anything. That was the moment I truly understood how deeply I needed to protect him, more than ever before.

CASE FILE# 000015

CASE MANAGER: BRIANNA BAIRD

LEAD AGENT: GORDON McCurr

SUBJECT: Angus O'Connor

It had been two weeks since I first brought up the topic of school and safety for Angus. My mind kept circling around one question—how could I truly keep him safe every day, especially when I wasn't around? I knew I needed a concrete plan, but every option seemed complicated or uncertain. I couldn't just rely on vague ideas; I had to come up with something solid. That's when I finally decided. I would ask the detectives he was closest to—those who knew him well and he trusted—to step in and help protect him. My hope was to start a rotation where each of them would be responsible for watching over Angus during school hours. I also planned for them to stay with him on

the weekends I was working. It felt
like a small, practical step in the
right direction, but it was also a big
relief to have a clear plan emerging.

The next day, I approached the
detectives whom Angus felt safest with. I
explained my idea, knowing how important it
was for him to have familiar faces nearby.
It was not easy, though, because I quickly
realized I didn't really know many of these
Constables and detectives as well as I would
like. Some of them I'd seen once or twice in
passing, and others I had only heard about.
I found it surprising how few of them I
could confidently say knew Angus personally.
Still, many of them listened carefully and
showed enthusiasm for the idea. They agreed
to take turns being his bodyguard for each
week, making sure he had someone watching
over him. They understood that Angus's
curiosity and tendency to find trouble meant
he needed more guidance. So, they decided it
would also be wise to teach him basic

self-defense skills—simple moves he could
use if he ever found himself in trouble and
no one was around to help.

Some of the detectives suggested little
things, like teaching him how to block a
punch or shout loudly for help if he felt
threatened. These skills wouldn't turn him
into a fighter, but they could give him
tools to stay safe. I appreciated their
thoughtful approach. It was clear they
understood that trusting someone with their
safety is more than just asking for help;
it's about giving them the skills to stand
their ground. We agreed that making sure

When it was finally time for Angus to
head to school. I couldn't shake the uneasy
twist that knotted inside me as I watched
him walk alongside Detective McAllister. The
two seemed wrapped up in their own world,
talking quietly as they headed in the
direction of the schoolyard. My mind was
pulled between concern and distraction,
fighting the urge to follow them or at least

keep a close eye. Instead, I forced myself
to push aside that gnawing suspicion and
turn my attention to the pile of case files
sprawled out on the table before me. I had
been too preoccupied to go through them
properly, constantly caught up in my
attempts to keep Angus close. Now, with a
heavy sigh, I reached out and opened the
very first file. My eyes immediately froze
on *that* name—GEOFFREY GOOSE. The name rang a
sharp, bitter note inside me, and I shivered
involuntarily. Seeing *that* name made me
remember how infamous he was in our little
town. The man was known for his complete
lack of intelligence; his nickname, "The
Brain of a Walnut," suited him perfectly.
Despite his evident shortcomings, Geoffrey
Goose had somehow managed to solve countless
thefts and armed robberies over the
years—cases that most detectives wouldn't
have been able to crack, or so they claimed.
I could hardly believe that a man so clearly
outmatched in basic common sense was the

same person credited with solving complicated crimes. I rolled my eyes at the absurdity of it all, but I kept reading through the files. Each page told a different story, some more disturbing than the last. I knew that behind that baffling reputation, Geoffrey Goose's work had real consequences, but it was difficult to take him seriously, especially given his personal failures. Yet somehow, he had gained respect in the department, and I wondered how that made sense. Did his strange methods really work, or was it all just shear dumb luck? My mind kept circling back to that question as I continued poring over the case records, trying to find some shred of truth amid the chaos.

I had spent what felt like hours sorting through a mountain of files and paperwork, each sheet representing another piece of a puzzle I was desperate to reconstruct. My attention was half-absorbed by the piles stacked high on the desk when

suddenly, the sharp chime of the rotary
phone echoed through the quiet hall. The
sound cut through the silence like a knife,
forcing my focus back to the present. I let
out a long, heavy sigh, before I reached out
and grasped the receiver. As I pressed it to
my ear, my ears caught a jarring
voice—urgent, snaky, filled with panic. It
was the detective, and his words hit me
instantly, shaking me from the fog of
fatigue. He explained how he had only turned
his back for a second, just a brief
moment—maybe a few seconds—and when he
turned back— I knew what he was saying—
Angus was gone. That innocent child, who had
barely made it into this world, was nowhere
to be found— again. His voice still trembled
from the rush of fear and worry, and I could
hear the desperation beneath it.

I sat there for a moment, staring at
the darkened wall, feeling a sense of
self-accusation and frustrated all at once.

The world was full of dangers, and children like Angus —so innocent—seemed to pay the highest price. I wondered how many others had suffered because of the cruelty hidden behind closed doors, behind locked windows and silent nights. It was frustrating to think about how such a young life could be caught in this web of violence and evil. And yet, I couldn't help but feel a sense of responsibility. Who else would stand up for him if not for people like me?

As I mulled over these dark thoughts, my mind drifted back to my father's words. I remembered that day clearly—how his voice had carried calm yet firm authority. He told me, "Life doesn't give us purpose. We give life purpose." Those words had settled deep in my mind. I knew what he meant—the idea that life isn't something we're handed, but something we create through our choices, our actions, our refusal to give in to despair. It reminded me of a verse he used to quote often, "For God has not given us a spirit of fear and timidity, but of power, love, and self-discipline (or a sound mind)" 2 Timothy 1:7 They were words I clung to when everything felt pointless. When I was overwhelmed with setbacks, when my goals seemed out of reach, and doubt crept in, I'd remember those words, and they'd pull me back. They reminded me that even amid the chaos, meaning wasn't just handed to us; we had to forge it ourselves. My mind pulled sharply back to the moment. I told the detective, who was waiting impatiently on the other end of the line, that I would be there shortly. Without wasting a second, I pushed myself up, hurriedly grabbed my coat, and dashed out of headquarters. Every step I took felt hurried but purposeful, pushing me to cover the short distance between our base and the school grounds faster. The chilly air hit my face as I ran, but I didn't slow down. It felt like time was slipping away, and I knew I had to get there quickly before

whatever needed my attention could unfold
further.

When I finally reached the school
grounds, I slowed down just enough to scan
my surroundings. My eyes searched for
Detective David McAllister, who I knew was
waiting for me near the back of the
building. The silence outside was almost
unnerving. Usually, the school grounds had
the hum of children playing or laughter
echoing, but today, everything was eerily
quiet. Only a faint whisper of wind brushed
past me, almost as if it was holding its
breath.

My eyes finally caught sight of
Detective McAllister. He was standing close
to Angus, who looked terrible — pale, drawn,
as if the shadow of death had brushed past
him, leaving behind a chill that couldn't be
shaken. I quickly moved to approach
McAllister, who seemed engaged in
conversation, but I called out clearly
enough to catch his attention. I asked him

to speak with me alone, wanting to hear what
he had to say without Angus listening in.
Angus understood instantly, nodding slowly,
as if he already knew I needed space.
Without hesitation, he turned and made his
way over to an old wooden bench a few yards
away. The bench looked weathered but sturdy,
and I watched him sit down quietly, our
brief visual exchange leaving silent shadows
behind us on the warm, quiet ground. The
moment felt heavy, loaded with unspoken
worries, and I wondered what secrets that
bench might hold if it could talk.

I asked McAllister to explain what
had occured. He looked agitated,
running a hand through his hair before
he spoke. He told me that Angus had
seen a man watching him through the
window of the school room and suffered
yet another panic attack. McAllister
said he had turned is back in hopes of
seeing the man and getting a
description of him but, when he looked

back at the window the man was gone, vanished with no clear sign as no one else had seen him. McAllister's voice was quiet but firm as he described the scene and how Angus had disappeared and had run off, not giving him the chance to see where he had run too.

I gently called Angus over, trying to sound calm and steady. He hesitated at first, still trembling from whatever had spooked him. When he reached me, I looked into his eyes, trying to understand what had made him so upset. I asked softly, "Who did you see" His small frame shivered as he gathered his thoughts. I could see he was fighting to stay composed, fighting against the fear that always seems to grip him tighter during these episodes. Then, with a shaky voice, he told me he saw a man staring at him in the window, how he thought he had seen him before but that he didn't know where he knew him from just that he felt incredibly scared. When I asked Angus to describe the man he said that the man had beady black eyes and was tall with reddish brown hair that hung in his eyes. I turned to look and McAllister and he shook his head saying that he didn't see anything out of the ordinary, making me wonder if Angus had really seen something or if he was just imagining it after his kidnapping weeks before. He went on to explain how it suddenly felt like there were invisible walls closing in around him, trapping him inside a tiny room with no way out. That feeling—like walls pressing tighter and tighter—made his chest ache and his breath become shallow. It was as if all the warmth, safety, and comfort he once knew were slipping away, leaving only this cold, suffocating space.These episodes can happen so quickly and seem to come out of nowhere, leaving Angus overwhelmed and confused. Anyone who's watched a loved one go through something like this might understand how helpless it feels, especially when Angus didn't fully understand what triggered it so often. This moment was difficult but revealing. It was a glimpse into what he experienced when his mind tangled with fear and memories that blurred reality.

A deep sigh escaped my lips as I decided he must have been imagining the man and stated as much to Angus who grew quieter in my presence. I realized this would not be a problem that could be fixed overnight.

I considered the best approach moving forward. Watching him every minute would be too risky and was honestly not possible, but simply ignoring what could be a problematic condition wouldn't help. That's when I decided it might be better if the detectives took turns watching Angus, perhaps even teaching him some of what they knew at headquarters and at home, so he could feel some sense of structure and safety while everything was in turmoil. I understood that placing him in headquarters wasn't without its dangers. The place was not always a safe zone, and there's always a chance of unexpected trouble breaking out. Still, I believed that having him nearby—under constant supervision-was the best way to keep a close eye on his health and his mental state, and perhaps my own sanity as well. We could monitor his reactions, see how he responded to different people and the environment, and hopefully spot signs of worsening stress or trauma early on.

Yet, making that move came with its own set of risks. Headquarters such as ours could be unpredictable and sometimes dangerous, especially if unrest flared up amongst the staff or if there were disagreements between the constables. But in this case, I was convinced that the chance of keeping Angus safe and making sure he received the right kind of attention was worth those risks.

About ten minutes later, we arrived at Headquarters. The building loomed ahead of us, its heavy doors a reminder of the many tough cases and emergencies that have taken place behind its walls. As we entered, I quickly found myself in the middle of a discussion. I laid out my plan to the chief inspector—the idea that different detectives could take shifts watching Angus, maybe even teach him some basic skills and schooling. The tone I used was firm but respectful; I knew that spending more time with him was essential.

Chief Inspector John Nobleman listened intently but appeared less than impressed. His face remained impassive, with that signature stern expression that he always wore. He rarely showed emotion unless it directly benefited him or suited his purpose. When I finished, I could see his mind quietly assessing the risks and benefits. His eyes, cold and calculating, seemed to weigh the proposal like a businessman analyzing a new deal. The truth was, Nobleman was a man known for his ruthless nature—someone willing to do

whatever it took to get results. He rarely
allowed any personal feelings to interfere
with his work. His ruthless reputation
matched his demeanor. It was almost ironic,
considering the rare moment of kindness he
had shown me. When he had allowed me to
focus solely on finding Angus after the
boy's sudden disappearance into the hands of
kidnappers, which stood out sharply against
his usual cold indifference. That was a
moment when even he put aside business for a
fleeting moment and showed a flicker of
compassion.

   Inspector Nobleman was visibly
irritated by the very idea that his
detectives might be caught doing anything
during work that didn't directly involve
closing a case or completing paperwork. He
believed every minute should be dedicated to
either gathering evidence, questioning
witnesses, or recording information relevant
to ongoing investigations. The notion that
they might waste time on activities outside

these strict boundaries, like chatting, taking breaks, or handling personal tasks, seemed to upset him deeply. It wasn't just a matter of wasting time in his eyes; he saw such distractions as a threat to the efficiency and seriousness of his team. He constantly emphasized the importance of focus and discipline, making it clear that the work they did was vital to solving crimes and keeping the streets safe.

Throughout many discussions with him, he expressed his concerns in detail. He was quick to question the purpose of even minor interruptions and it was a challenge to convince him otherwise. When suggestions were made that some downtime or casual interactions with Angus could build rapport and improve teamwork, he dismissed them, insisting that such things only create opportunities for mistakes or a loss of focus. After explaining repeatedly that the activities in question would not interfere with their investigations, and reassuring

193

him multiple times that his detectives would remain fully committed to their duties, I had to emphasize that the proposed activities were purely administrative. They were scheduled in a way that would not hinder the progress of any case. I explained that these moments of light activity could help the detectives in the long run—by preventing fatigue and helping them stay sharp—without diminishing their effectiveness on the job. It was a hard won argument, but one that took logic and clarity to reach such a man who valued discipline above all else.

CASE FILE#000016

CASE MANAGER: BRIANNA BAIRD

LEAD AGENT: GORDON McCurr

SUBJECT: Angus O'Connor

A few days went by in a blur of busy
lessons as we finally began Angus's
relentless schedule of learning. His lessons
covered everything from basic arithmetic to
the classics of literature, from scientific
facts to the art of self-defense. It was
clear that these lessons were not just
casual drills but a continuous effort to
improve him in many areas. Several
detectives had generously offered to help
teach most of these lessons during the week.
Most managed to keep their detective work,
investigations, case reports, and other
assignments up to date and separate from the
tutoring sessions.

However, not every detective was able to draw that line easily. A few of them found it challenging to keep their detective duties completely separate from Angus's education. They often blurred the lines, letting their cases intrude into lessons, leading to distraction and confusion. The chief inspector paid close attention to how things were progressing. His patience wore thin when he saw these mixed-ups happen more frequently. He was quick to notice that some detectives weren't doing their best to keep things separate. His anger only intensified because the station was just now starting to earn the publics respect despite the turmoil caused by the Whitechapel murders, which have, in some ways, been glorified by parts of the public. Ever since those grisly crimes, the station had lost many good men. The inspector had personally overseen the restructuring, making sure every detail was perfect. The cases involving Whitechapel are still open, and I suspect that they will

remain open for years unless there is new
evidence. I vaguely remember something about
the cases that might be similar to Iris
O'Connor's case. The symbols might have been
seen near the victims, but I was ordered to
leave Whitechapel out of my current
investigation as the inspector was paranoid
about anything that might disrupt the
carefully crafted press release that
happened months ago. Inspector Nobleman
viewed the distractions from the detectives
cases and the interference with Angus's
lessons as a threat to the station's
hard-earned stability.

After a long and exhausting argument
between Nobleman and I where we discussed
the lack of focus among the detectives, we
reached a decision that would shape the days
ahead for Angus. We agreed that he would
have his lessons during the evening hours,
giving him enough time to focus without
distractions. During the daytime, he would
lend a hand at Headquarters, helping out

with various tasks. It wasn't an easy choice
to make, especially considering how much
worry there was about placing a
twelve-year-old in such a position.
Inspector Nobleman was hesitant at first due
to Angus's current emotional state and the
psychological affect of his mothers murder
causing a sort of age regression within him,
along with knowing everything that had
happened to him it made Agnus seem younger
and frailer than he truly was. In the end,
it took both myself and Detective McAllister
to convince Inspector Nobleman of the
importance of stability in Angus's life,
especially given the strange circumstances
he often found himself in.

A few weeks passed since they began the
new routine of giving Angus lessons in the
evening while he helped out during the day.
During that time, subtle but noticeable
changes became clear. We started to see
Angus becoming more confident. His attitude
toward work had shifted, and he began

solving problems more on his own without
constantly asking for help. What was most
striking was how his ability to perform his
tasks and his attention to detail improved
day by day. It was as if he was growing more
capable with each passing week. The progress
in his schoolwork was clear; he was
completing assignments faster, and his
understanding of complex problems improved.
No longer did he need as much help from
others to complete his lessons, which was a
relief to everyone who cared about him.
The change was not limited to Angus alone.
We also observed a shift in the atmosphere
around the chief inspector. Before Angus
started working with him during the day, the
inspector had been more reserved and stern,
often giving off an air of coldness. His
commands were sharp, and he seemed distant.
Now, somewhat unexpectedly, the inspector's
demeanor softened. He appeared less detached
and more approachable. Small gestures, like
offering encouraging words or giving a

reassuring nod, became more common. It was as if the bond growing between Angus and the inspector was melting some of the chill that had long surrounded him. The relationship, initially filled with formality and distance, was now showing signs of genuine connection. It was clear that working alongside Angus was having a positive impact on both of them.

None of the detectives had any clue about what Angus was doing with the chief inspector behind closed doors. It was a mystery that hung in the air, silent and unresolved. The only thing I knew for sure was what Angus had told me. He said he was learning a lot from the chief inspector, gaining insights that others couldn't see. That one simple statement made me wonder if Angus was secretly being mentored, not in the usual formal way, but in a more personal, perhaps even unconventional manner. Many of us thought about this closely, trying to piece together what might

be happening. Some of us even believed that
Angus might be getting private lessons on
being a detective — maybe in ways he
couldn't or wouldn't share openly. The idea
that he was breaking down the barriers that
the chief inspector usually kept up warmed
my heart, and it brought comfort to my
colleagues as well. We saw it as a sign of
trust and progress.

Meanwhile, Angus himself had changed so
much. When I first met him, he was a fragile
boy—so thin he looked like he might blow
away in a stiff wind. But now, there was a
different strength to him. His muscles had
developed, proof of the physical effort he
had put in. You could tell he was starting
to rebuild himself, both on the outside and
deep inside. He was no longer the boy who
shied away from facing his fears and demons.
The nightmares that haunted him in the early
days had begun to fade; they no longer
controlled him. Instead, they were replaced
by much rarer flashbacks, which would come

unexpectedly but less often than before. His panic attacks, once so frequent and intense, now rarely visited him. It was a slow but steady improvement. The nights were still a challenge—he was easily startled by loud noises or sudden movements—but that was to be expected. You could see the effort he put into healing, into stabilizing himself. I wondered if this internal drive could be connected with his own desire to find his mother's killer.

CASE FILE#000017

CASE MANAGER: BRIANNA BAIRD

LEAD AGENT: GORDON McCurr

SUBJECT: Angus O'Connor

It was late one evening when Angus was working through his nightly lessons. His focus was sharp, but I quickly noticed something unusual. Watching him, I realized he was breezing through the work with an ease that seemed almost effortless. I knew at that moment we couldn't continue to give him the same level of assignments. His mind was expanding so quickly that he was outgrowing the middle-level tasks I had carefully chosen for him. It became clear that I needed to find ways to push him harder. I had to get more creative if I wanted to keep him engaged and ensure his growth continued. I started looking for more complex material—topics that would stretch his abilities and make him think deeper and more critically. I considered advanced puzzles, more challenging math problems, or even creative writing assignments that would require more insight. I knew he was capable of much more, and I had to keep him motivated before he lost interest or, worse, grew apathetic.

His training was not limited to academics alone. His self-defense lessons were also progressing remarkably well. Angus had shown a natural talent for physical agility and quick thinking, which made me more confident in his ability to defend himself if needed. Over the past eight weeks, I watched him learn to outmaneuver most of our top Constables in just a matter of minutes. His rapid progress was impressive. He was mastering techniques that had taken others months to grasp. For example, he could now evade a mock attack smoothly, using clever footwork and strategic moves that made his opponents struggle to keep up. It was a relief to see him so capable in this area, especially because it meant I no longer had to worry as much about him being vulnerable. What mattered most to me was the part these lessons played in his safety. With the amount of dangerous individuals who might be after the last C'Connor family member, of which I had a dozen leads, each more concerning than the last. The faster Angus learned to defend himself, the better I felt about his chances of staying safe. In the end, his progress in both academics and self-defense was giving me confidence that he was growing stronger, smarter, and more prepared to face whatever dangers might, or should I say will come his way.

Aaric MacKenzie was our biggest lead and my biggest fear. He wasn't just a suspect; he was the one name that haunted every report and whispered fear throughout the city. Aaric had a long history that made his name synonymous with darkness. Everyone knew he was a psychopath—a person with no empathy, no remorse, and a thirst for pandemonium. His reputation was built on a string of brutal murders that seemed to grow more horrifying with each passing year. Detectives had tried to get close to him many times, but every attempt ended in disaster.

Aaric had a chilling knack for evading capture. Whenever law enforcement thought they were onto something, he disappeared like a ghost. No one had ever caught him in the act, but the evidence left behind painted a clear and terrifying picture. His victims were often found in the most horrifying and unimaginable conditions soaked in darkness and screaming of pure evil. He showed a complete lack of human emotion and decency.

Over the years, rumors spread about Aaric's motives and methods. People said he was born with a twisted mind, perhaps scarred by a troubled past or driven by some unseen darkness. The sheer brutality of his crimes made him a figure of fear, almost

mythic in the way he remained just out of
reach. All of Scotland Yard knew that
catching him was the key to ending the
terror that gripped the community. But each
time they thought they had a lead, Aaric
would strike again, vanishing into the
shadows before anyone could get close
enough. No one knew what exactly drove him
or how he chose his targets. What made him
stand apart was his ability to move
seamlessly between life and death, always
one step ahead of the law. Every time
someone came close, they paid the price—with
the evidence of a sick mind behind it all.
It became clear that Aaric MacKenzie was
more than just a killer; he was a spawn of
madness, a living nightmare, and catching
him had become a quest that haunted
Headquarters every waking moment.

This was why Aaric MacKenzie was our most
significant lead. Tracking him down meant
facing a villain who had eluded justice for

years. The danger was real, the stakes high, and the threat he posed to everyone couldn't be overstated. He was a living reminder that some monsters refuse to stay hidden forever, and stopping him was more than just a case; it was a race against the very darkness that threatened to swallow everything.

CASE FILE# 000018

CASE MANAGER: BRIANNA BAIRD

LEAD AGENT: GORDON McCurr

SUBJECT: ANGUS O'Connor

It was a day everyone wished they could
erase from memory. The moment everything
finally unraveled after months of effort.
All the detectives and investigators
involved had worked tirelessly, each of us
pitching in to teach Angus—our young
apprentice—what we knew. We had hoped that,
with time, he would sharpen his skills and
become a true part of our team, but now it
all seemed pointless. Everything was
spiraling out of control, slipping through
our fingers like grains of sand. I'd just
received crushing news — a critical lead
that could have widened the search for Aaric
MacKenzie had fallen apart just when we
thought we were getting close. The woman who
spoke to me all those months ago had been

the key to narrowing down his last known whereabouts, yet now she was gone, taken from us as if she never existed.

I felt a sharp sting of frustration and despair, emotions that tensed my shoulders and made my fists clench so tightly I thought they might burst. Aaric MacKenzie, the man who seemed to always stay one step ahead, had once again claimed yet another life. The weight of that fact pressed down on me like an anvil, heavy enough to crush my spirit. It was like watching a man drown while you stood helpless, knowing every second that slipped by might be the last. That fury—anger so raw it burned—boiled over inside me. I couldn't stand it anymore. I stormed into the house with no regard for anything else. The mahogany door of my room shuddered violently on its hinges as I threw it open, the sound an unnecessary punctuation mark on my already ragged state I didn't notice the faint, fearful whimper from my ward's face and the way their body

stiffened with dread or the detective
following me. My emotions clouded everything
else. Without thinking, I pushed past all
the clutter in the hall, my mind consumed by
only one thought: justice must be served. I
tore upstairs, my footsteps heavy, and threw
open the door to my room with a loud bang.

Inside, I sank onto the bed, trying
desperately to calm myself. My chest heaved
with the effort to regain control. My mind
raced, replaying the moments when I had been
close to a breakthrough but now found myself
engulfed in darkness.I pulled in a sharp
breath, forcing the cold Scottish air from
the open window down into my chest. One
inhale hit hard, then another followed,
filling my lungs with the crisp chill that
bit at my throat. The wind outside howled
against the stone walls of the old house,
carrying hints of heather and damp earth
from the moors. It grounded me, this air,
sharp and real, cutting through the fog in
my head. The clock on the mantel ticked on,

each second a loud jab. Its wooden face, carved with faded Celtic knots, had watched over my family for generations. Now it mocked me, counting out the hours I had lost in doubt and delay. Aaric had taken more than time—he had twisted it, turning simple days into a web of suspicion and fear. His schemes had pulled us all into this mess, leaving scars that no calendar could erase. Control, I told myself, gripping the edge of the oak table until my knuckles turned white. You must hold on to control. Let it slip, and everything crumbles. Angus needed me steady. He paced the room earlier, asking questions I could not answer yet, his trust hanging on my every word. He depended on my clear head to guide us through the storm Aaric had stirred.

Slowly, the red haze began to recede. The pounding in my temples softened to a dull ache. I pushed myself up, smoothing the wrinkles from my waistcoat, trying to reassemble the facade of the infallible

investigator. I needed to descend, to speak
with Angus and the others, to lay out a new
plan, a new strategy to ensnare the elusive
MacKenzie.I took a tentative step toward the
door, my focus entirely on the cold, hard
logic required for the coming discussion.
But I never reached the threshold.

A sudden, firm pressure clamped around my
right arm, halting me mid-stride. It wasn't
a rough grab, but it was absolute—a tether
designed to prevent further movement. I
turned, my jaw tight, ready to unleash a
fresh wave of frustration on whoever dared
impede my path. The words died unspoken. It
was Detective Jacob McNamara. He towered
over me by a good six inches. His lean body
stayed stiff, like a board. Bright brown
eyes stared out, a bit bigger through the
round glass of his specs. He had just turned
twenty. But right then, he carried the
weight of someone twice his age. It came
from years of hard knocks in a rough town,
where kids learned early to spot lies and

call out wrongs. Folks like him judged the world quick and sharp, based on scars from broken homes and bad choices around them.

I opened my mouth to argue. Not even a word out yet, Jacob's other hand flew forward fast. His fingers gripped the stiff collar of my shirt. He squeezed tight, enough to yank me off my feet. Balance gone, I stumbled back. Then he pushed. The force felt soft at first, but it built strong with no way to fight it, my back hit the thick wooden doorframe hard. The collision jarred my teeth, driving the air from my lungs in a startled gasp. Jacob didn't release the collar; he held me pinned, his face inches from mine. The protective edge I knew he possessed—the fierce loyalty he showed for Angus—was now honed into a weapon pointed directly at me. I could read the tight, unforgiving lines around his mouth, the almost imperceptible narrowing of his eyes that signaled danger. He wasn't yelling; he didn't need to. His presence was the accusation. Then, just as swiftly as he had restrained me, he released my collar. The moment he let go, he stepped away, his movements slow and deliberate, a predator circling its prey. He walked to the door, his back to me, and with a soft, decisive click that seemed deafening in the sudden silence, he engaged the heavy brass bolt.

Fear, cold and sharp, finally pierced through the lingering remnants of my rage. I was trapped. Jacob turned back, walking toward me with that same measured, purposeful stride. The cool detachment that usually characterized his demeanor had been stripped away, replaced by a terrifying, quiet fury. His eyes, usually so clear and analytical, were smoldering. He stopped a few feet away, hands clasped loosely behind his back, looking less like a detective and more like a judge about to deliver a sentence. His voice, when it finally came, was a low, steady rumble, stripped of all warmth. It was the sound of bedrock shifting.

"You," Jacob began, his gaze unwavering, "are a man obsessed with justice. You chase it through the darkest corners of this city, yet you fail to see the wreckage you create in your own home. You have lost your center, and you need to find it again. I know you are a Godly man but you are blinded to the consequences of your actions. What was the verse you shared with me when we first met? *A wrathful man stirs up strife, but he who is slow to anger allays contention.'* *Proverbs 15:18.* You are stirring up strife all around you, and you do not even recognize it."

I opened my mouth to defend myself, to shout about Aaric, about the latest victim, about the necessity of my rage. Jacob cut me off instantly, the sheer force of his controlled anger silencing me more effectively than any shout. "Do not speak of Aaric MacKenzie, not now. Not when the consequence of your temper is still trembling downstairs." He took one step closer, forcing me to lean back against the doorframe. "That sound, McCurr," he spat, "that deafening crash when you slammed the door—it was not just noise. It was a catalyst. It was a hammer blow against the fragile structure we have spent months rebuilding."

My heart dropped, a cold weight replacing the burning fury. I knew, deep inside, that my storming in had been reckless, but I hadn't let myself truly consider the impact.

"Angus… was… making… progress," Jacob stated, the silence between each word amplifying the accusation. "He was talking, he was eating, he was starting to trust that the world outside was not perpetually violent. And you, in your righteous fury, ripped that thin veil away. What does the bible say in Psalms 82? It says: *Defend the poor and fatherless; Do justice to the afflicted and needy. Deliver the poor and needy; Free them from the hand of the wicked.* Angus needs protection and love, he does not need *your* anger."

He paused, letting the full horror sink in. "He is downstairs now, sir. McCallum and McCarry are trying to coax him back from a night that happened months ago. Your dramatic entrance sent him straight back to that hallway, straight back to the night he watched his mother..." Jacob stopped, unable to finish the sentence, but the implication hung heavy and suffocating in the air.

The realization hit me with the force of a physical blow. I hadn't just caused a disturbance; I had inflicted a serious wound. I had actively undone the healing. "I—I didn't mean to… I didn't think it was still that bad," I stammered, the words hollow and inadequate.

Jacob's lips curled into a tight, disgusted line. "That is precisely the problem, isn't it? You didn't think. You allowed your vendetta to blind you to the needs of the one person you swore to protect. You have allowed yourself to see only the grand scale of justice, while ignoring the small, crucial battles being fought right under your roof."

He leaned in, his voice dropping to an almost inaudible whisper, yet every syllable was razor-sharp. "If you cannot learn to temper your reactions, if you cannot prioritize the stability of that boy over the pursuit of a ghost, then perhaps you are not fit to be his guardian. You are not just failing the case; you are destroying him and you are distancing yourself from the God whom you love so much."

The accusation was worse than any physical reprimand. It was the truth, spoken plainly and brutally. *Iron Sharpens Iron.* My stomach clenched with a sudden, overwhelming wave of guilt and fear. Had I really pushed him that far back? Was all the work, all the tentative steps toward recovery, undone because of my arrogance and my temper? I knew what the answer was and I knew then how much I had failed Angus in that moment.

Jacob straightened, his posture returning to its customary severity. He looked at me for one last agonizing moment, his eyes communicating a profound disappointment that cut deeper than his anger. "Go downstairs," he commanded, his voice returning to its normal, soft, authoritative tone. "Look at what happened. And for Angus's sake, contain yourself. Pray before you speak, think before you act." He unlocked the door with a sharp thunk of the bolt and stepped aside. I moved mechanically, my feet heavy, the weight of Jacob's words pressing down on me. The descent down the staircase felt endless, each step bringing me closer to the evidence of my failure. The drawing-room was quiet, save for the low, soothing murmur of voices. When I stepped inside, the scene was exactly as Jacob had described, and yet far worse than I had imagined.

Angus was seated on the edge of the sofa, stiff and rigid, his body trembling visibly beneath his tweed jacket. His breath was coming in short, shallow, ragged gasps—hyperventilating, the frantic rhythm of a man drowning in air. Detective McCarry sat beside him, speaking softly about the weather, about anything mundane, trying to anchor him to the present. McCallum knelt opposite, gently guiding Angus's hands, trying to encourage him to slow his breathing.

Angus's face was deathly pale, his features drawn tight with terror. His sea-green eyes were wide, vacant, staring past us at something only he could see. It was the look of pure, primal fear, a flicker of memory flashing—the horror of that night, the hallway, the blood, the loss—all resurrected by the sound of a simple, slammed door. I stood frozen for a moment, the guilt a searing brand on my soul. I had done this.

It took several excruciating minutes,
filled only with the sound of Angus's
desperate breathing and the quiet,
persistent voices of the detectives, before
the trembling began to subside. Slowly,
agonizingly, Angus's eyes lost their vacant
stare. His breathing deepened, though it
still hitched occasionally. When he finally
looked up, his gaze swept over the room,
avoiding mine until the last possible
moment. When our eyes finally met, a
palpable wave of emotion passed between us:
fear from him, and a crushing sense of guilt
from me. He flinched, a tiny, involuntary
movement that was nevertheless a punch to my
gut. It was a retreat, a confirmation that I
was the source of his pain.

I moved forward slowly, carefully,
dropping to my knees on the thick carpet
before the sofa. I ignored the protesting
creak of my joints, focusing entirely on the
boy. I kept my voice low, stripped of all

the bombast and fury that had consumed me
upstairs.

"Angus," I began, my voice rough with
remorse. I looked directly into his
still-terrified eyes, making sure he saw
nothing but sincerity in mine. "I am so
sorry."

He blinked, his gaze remaining fixed on
my face, waiting.

"I lost control," I admitted, the words
tasting bitter as they passed my lips. "I
let my anger run wild, and I did not think—I
did not consider the terror that sound must
have caused you." I reached out slowly,
tentatively, and placed my hand on the sofa
near his knee, not touching him, but
offering a silent anchor.
"That noise," I continued, keeping my tone
steady and quiet, "it must have sounded like
an eruption. Like a storm breaking right
here, pulling you back into a place you
should never have to revisit. I was

reckless, and I terrified you. For that, I have no excuse."

He swallowed hard, his throat bobbing. He was still too dazed to speak, but he was listening.

"I owe you an explanation, not to excuse my behavior, but so you understand the source of my foolish rage." I leaned forward slightly. "It was Aaric MacKenzie. We were close—so close to finding the location, to finding answers about your mother's death." My voice tightened, but I kept it low. "And he slipped away again. He claimed another victim, another life, and vanished into the fog of the night. The trail went cold, Angus. Completely cold." I clenched my hand into a fist on the sofas fabric. "That frustration… that helplessness… it boiled over. Every dead end is a blow. Every time he escapes, it feels like I am failing you and your mother all over again. I am angry because I feel useless, trapped, watching injustice walk free when I swore I would stop it."

I met his gaze again, hoping he saw the depth of the commitment beneath the failure. "I feel the weight of that promise every day, and knowing that her case remains open, unresolved, that I am no closer to giving her peace—you peace... it grates on me."

I waited, letting the silence absorb the confession. Angus finally shifted, a tiny, almost imperceptible movement. He lifted his head slightly and gave a slow, deliberate nod. It wasn't forgiveness, perhaps, but it was acknowledgment. He understood the pain of the chase, the agony of the unresolved tragedy. We stayed there, me kneeling on the floor, him on the sofa, the truth of our shared trauma hanging between us. In that quiet room, surrounded by the men who protected him, I saw clearly what Jacob had forced me to confront. The fight for justice against Aaric MacKenzie was vital, but the fight to keep Angus whole, to protect his peace, was paramount.

The door slamming had been a thunderclap in his world. I had to be the steady hand, the quiet reassurance, not the source of the storm. I knew then that every step forward I took in the case must be measured not just by clues found, but by the stability I maintained for the boy whose life depended on it.

CASE FILE# 000019

CASE MANAGER: BRIANNA BAIRD

LEAD AGENT: GORDON McCurr

SUBJECT: Angus O'Connor

Days had passed since Angus experienced that terrifying flashback, and the toll of that moment was still clear in every part of him. He couldn't bring himself to meet my gaze; his eyes remained averted, as if the world had suddenly become too much to face. His nightmares had returned with a vengeance, plaguing our nights without mercy. The dark circles under his eyes grew darker and more pronounced, sharp shadows that contrasted sharply with his piercing sea-green eyes—eyes once full of life, now overshadowed by exhaustion and fear. It was as if someone had drained all the color and light from his face, leaving behind a ghost of the boy I once knew.

I had thrown myself back into work, trying to drown out the worry I felt for

him. My focus was on finding Aaric
MacKenzie, the suspect at the center of our
investigation, and that effort kept my mind
from spiraling into darker places. I hoped
that if I could find Aaric, if I could solve
Iris's murder, then Angus would be fine,
that my one moment my one mistake would be
erased and all of the progress Angus had
made would be there again. Until then, I
couldn't face him. I would wake up before
Angus even stirred, praying for a new lead
and asking God for guidance before quietly
slipping out of bed to begin my day. Then
I'd come home after he had gone to bed,
feeling as if I was missing out on him
entirely—like he was slipping further away
with each passing hour. During the day, the
detectives from McNamara's team stepped in
to stay with Angus, taking turns to watch
over him. None of us wanted to leave him
alone for very long, knowing how fragile he
had become. McCallum, who usually kept a
tough front, surprised us all by showing

genuine concern. He made sure Angus wasn't left unattended, sitting with him and offering words of reassurance and courage. Even Chief Inspector Nobleman, lent his presence and patience, spending time tutoring Angus through simple tasks and listening as Angus fought to tell his story—though the words often seemed to get caught in his throat.

Being confined to this small, secluded space was lonely. There were no quick visits or casual chats, only quiet moments where my thoughts tended to consume me. But the isolation made it easier to stay focused on what I was sure mattered most: finding Aaric MacKenzie and bringing him to justice. I didn't have time for anything else, not even to check on Angus during those long days. Colleagues pushed me to spend time with him, insisting it could help. They said he needed someone, anyone, to break through that wall of silence and fear. But I refused, knowing that I was the catalyst in this relapse, I refused to see what was truly happening beneath his distant stare.

Now, looking back, I realize I missed the signs. I wish I had paid closer attention to the subtle details—those small cues that someone might miss in life's whirlwind. If I had, I would have seen the shatter in his eyes, the flicker of despair and helplessness that now haunts me. I would have noticed how gaunt his cheeks had become, as if he'd lost more weight than I realized. The pale hue of his skin looked almost transparent, like he was fading away, piece by piece. Those days of separation kept me blind to the real damage happening inside him, damage that words couldn't easily explain, nor could I fully comprehend at the time. Time has given me some clarity now, but back then, I was only focused on the case. I thought I was doing the right thing—concentrating all my energy on justice and on finding Aaric. Still, the cost was clear, and I regret that. Because if I had

seen what was really going on, I might have
done something more to help. Maybe then, I
would have noticed the worn look behind his
eyes, the fragile state his mind and body
had fallen into, and I wouldn't have let him
slip so far away.

When I finally arrived home late that
night, I was unprepared for what I found.
The sitting room was packed with detectives,
many I recognized from past cases, all of
them standing quietly but with tense, grim
faces. They had been there for hours,
tending to Angus, who was resting in the
corner, looking drained but more alert. In
the midst of them stood Chief Inspector
Nobleman, his stern expression hard and
cold. His eyes seemed to cut through the dim
light as he looked in my direction, and I
could tell that he was furious. The weight
of their expressions pressed down on me,
making me feel as if I had stepped into a
storm I couldn't escape. That image suddenly
transported me back to my first day at

training with Scotland Yard. I remembered how nervous I had been, how every new step felt like a mountain to climb. Now, standing in the shadow of those seasoned detectives, I realized how far I had come but also how much work I still had ahead.

Taking a deep breath, I forced myself to stay calm. My heart pounded, but I kept my face steady. Carefully, I stepped into the room, trying to look confident even though a thousand questions looped in my mind. I surveyed the scene—detectives whispering to each other, glancing my way with cautious suspicion, and Angus staring , his eyes flickering with a mixture of worry and hope. The air felt heavy, thick with unspoken tensions, and I knew I had to choose my words wisely.

Chief Inspector Nobleman was the first to approach me. Each step he took radiated authority and contained a hint of anger that I could feel coursing through him. His voice was clipped, firm. He told me plainly, with no room for arguing, that I would be working with Angus alone for the next two weeks. The goal was to rebuild the trust that had been broken, slowly, carefully. I could see the disappointment and frustration simmering behind his eyes as he spoke. It was clear he didn't trust me right now, and I couldn't blame him. Trust was fragile, especially in our line of work. I knew that gaining Angus's trust back wouldn't be easy, nor would it happen overnight. I stared as Nobleman and the others left in quiet fury, part of me wishing I could leave with them.

As much as I missed Angus and his familiar presence,—I understood this wasn't about longing or regret. It was about proving myself. I was painfully aware of the hurt I had caused him, the look in his eyes when he felt betrayed. That look haunted me. I hated to see it, and I knew I would have to face it directly if I wanted to earn his trust again. The thought of meeting his watchful, guarded gaze made me shiver. I wasn't sure whether I was more afraid of failing or of breaking him even further. Still, I realized I had no choice but to do this. For Angus, and for myself. The next two weeks were filled with small steps—building bridges where trust had been broken, patching wounds that hadn't yet healed. I stared at him for a long moment, knowing I had a lot of work ahead—and that, for now, silence was the only option.

When I felt like the world was crumbling beneath my feet, I prayed, I prayed for guidance, for forgiveness, for patience and for love. I pleaded with God to have another chance to fix the rift I had caused between Angus and myself. I felt the claws of grief grip me as I sat hunched over before the fire and the small spark of hope I had felt two weeks ago began to disappear, it was then that a small hand was on my shoulder, I jerked up and saw Angus standing there, tears in his eyes, and for the first time in months he looked me in the eye and in a soft whisper he said the words I never thought I'd hear again.

"I love you."

I didn't know how to respond. I had never expected to hear him say that again, not after I had pushed him away. Angus continued to speak in a soft quiet voice.

"I have faith that God will help us find my mother's killer. In God's time, not in our own. After all, mother used to quote Jeremiah 29:11 when she felt lost after father disappeared. *'For I know the Plans I have for you, declares the Lord. Plans to prosper you, and not to harm you. Plans for Hope and a future.'* God will see it through."

I was stunned, here was Angus, a young boy who had been through more in the last year than most have been in their whole lives and he still had hope. Hope that God would see it through. And somehow, knowing that made it easier for me to see it to. We may not have caught the killer yet, but one

day we would, even if we didn't know where
to start. And we would do it together.

Five Years Later- POST SCRIPT

The case had gone cold. No new leads, no fresh evidence, no way to connect what happened that night to anyone. Mrs. O'Connor's murder remained unsolved, buried in a pile of dead ends. The trail had gone cold so deeply that even the sharpest minds at Scotland Yard couldn't find a way forward. It was as if the case had disappeared into an abyss, leaving behind only questions and faint hopes that someday, someone might crack it open again.

Meanwhile, Angus has grown into a tall, quiet seventeen-year-old. Though still young, he's been given a major role—he's now working for Headquarters. When he told me, I couldn't help but shake, feeling a mix of pride and unease. I wasn't expecting him to walk that path so soon, especially not after everything that happened. Many of us at the Yard had watched over him, shaping him into the person he is today, guiding him through patrols, training, and quiet lessons in deduction. It's clear he inherited more than just our skills; he inherited our burdens, too. There's a part of me that's proud to see him stepping into this world, but I also know that the wounds he carries—hidden behind that calm face—are still fresh. You can't see them, but they're there. Tears behind his eyes, scars that don't fade. They don't close up even after years of pain. Sometimes, you catch a glimpse of them in the way he hesitates before speaking or his quiet, distant stare that seems to look right through you.

CASE UPDATE:

There's been a new lead, a faint but promising trace, on Aaric. And surprisingly, there's also a new thread to follow in the case of Mrs. O'Connor's murder. Someone has pushed open the door again, asking questions we thought were long gone. A break has been made in the code found at the scene of Iris

O'Connor's murder, a solid lead that could help break the case open. Even more surprising is that the case has been reopened and assigned to someone very familiar—Angus C'Connor himself. The boy who once sat silent in the back of the room, listening to stories of detectives and darkness, is now the one digging through the shadows. It's hard not to wonder if this is the break we needed all along. After years of silence, the pieces could finally start to fall into place. Or maybe not. It is a reminder that no mystery is ever truly closed. Not until every secret sees the light. And maybe, just maybe, Angus is the one who will finally close this chapter. Maybe he will find the answers we couldn't.

Time will tell...

Detective Gordon McCurr

Detective Gordon McCurr

www.ingramcontent.com/pod-product-compliance
Lightning Source LLC
Chambersburg PA
CBHW051105030726
47504CB00006B/1795